Mismatch

Alyssa Madder

Copyright © 2023 by Alyssa Madder

All rights reserved.

No portion of this book may be reproduced in any form without written permission from the publisher or author, except as permitted by U.S. copyright law.

Contents

1. Introduction ... 1
2. Meeting ... 13
3. First Encounter ... 27
4. Deep Understanding ... 43
5. Falling in Love ... 58
6. The Dance ... 77
7. The Eventual Talk ... 103
8. Secrets Revealed ... 119
9. Invitation ... 140
10. Party and Betrayal ... 158
11. The Fight ... 172
12. Family is Family ... 186
13. The Ultimate Truth ... 198

14.	Arrest and Sentence	218
15.	Parents	241
16.	Happily Ever After	262
17.	Epilogue	281

Contents

1. Introduction — 1
2. Meeting — 13
3. First Encounter — 27
4. Deep Understanding — 43
5. Falling in Love — 58
6. The Dance — 77
7. The Eventual Talk — 103
8. Secrets Revealed — 119
9. Invitation — 140
10. Party and Betrayal — 158
11. The Fight — 172
12. Family is Family — 186
13. The Ultimate Truth — 198

14.	Arrest and Sentence	218
15.	Parents	241
16.	Happily Ever After	262
17.	Epilogue	281

Introduction

Chapter 1

"Stop sulking, Alison," her mother muttered disapprovingly. Alison shrugged and gazed mutely at the scenery outside the plane window. She was angry, yes, but she didn't have the courage to go up against her tigress mother who had once taken Taekwondo classes back in Japan. It wasn't her fault her parents had to choose this time of the year to move all the way across the globe to the US. Just because they felt stifled by the Japanese society didn't meant that they had to do something so drastic. Couldn't they have just moved to some nearer- Africa- maybe? She would probably have had more fun playing with the hyenas than staying in boring old US.

"America is your homeland, dearest, you should never forget that."

That was one of her mother's all-too-typical phrases. True, she was technically born in America but she had been living in Japan for twelve years. And while the Japanese typically didn't approve of Caucasians in the country, she could fit in pretty well in school despite being part of the minority. Alison had once read about mean high school girls in those romance novels she bought and she wasn't too pleased to find herself in the shoes of the new girl- vulnerable and susceptible to the teasing and bullying.

"Alison, look at that pretty bird!" Her sister, Carrie, who was two years younger than her, pointed at a magnificent eagle which was gazing curiously at them as it flapped its arch wings. Alison sighed once more. Even Carrie seemed excited about enrolling in an American high school but probably because she had a thing for American guys.

"Look, what's our school's name again?" Alison asked morosely.

"Cornwall Institution! Isn't that just so cool? " Carrie gushed happily and her sister rolled her eyes. Alison didn't like the name. It sounded way too old-fashioned. She liked her old school which was called "Seifu Senior High School" in Kyoto. That sounded more refined and elegant and besides, everyone was always sunnily polite there.

"Where are we staying, Dad?" Carrie shook her father who was flipping through a Sports magazine and he didn't look all too pleased to be interrupted during his leisure time.

"Some flat in Seattle," he grunted.

Some flat in Seattle? Alison had a vision of some rundown apartment with cracks and paint peeling off the walls and she grimaced. She wanted to remain in the large spacious traditional house that they had rented in Japan which was called Machiya. They even had a small little garden and a pond where she reared some goldfish. Why were her parents sacrificing all these luxuries to stay in one of those box rooms with nothing but skyscrapers in the background?

"Look Alison," her mother said softly. "I know it's more difficult for you than the rest of us- leaving your friends behind and having to start afresh again." Alison listened quietly, wondering what her mother was implying. She continued, "And I want you to know that we didn't leave Japan because we hated it but because we want you to grow up in a place where you can truly be someone you are."

"I can do that in Japan. I feel like a Japanese already! Why can't we apply for a Japanese citizenship? I don't want to be an American!" Alison blurted out and blushed. She wasn't used to talking back to her mother. In Japan, they were always expected to address their parents all the time. Somehow, the idea of going to a foreign land had made her shed off all those customs she had learnt during her childhood. That made her even more pissed.

"Alison." Her mother looked worry and tired and for a moment there, she looked much older than usual. "What's the point of obtaining a Japanese citizenship when we can have an American one?" Alison flinched. Having those words said out loud made her parents' decision to move to Washington more final than anything.

"Enough, Alison," her father's voice thundered which invited curious stares from a few Chinese passengers sitting in front of them. They strained their necks and withdrew back when they caught sight of her father's irritated face. "You will not contest our decision and I expect you to follow your mother's orders," he spoke sharply.

Military General. Alison thought. She had a resentful relationship with her father in particular because she couldn't quite agree with whatever ideology he thinks of. For a start, her father had been brought up in a strict and reserved family who wasn't accustomed to expressing their own feelings. Her grandparents were the finest examples of why her father turned out to be such a cold and overbearing person.

"I'm sorry, Father," she whispered. This seemed to please her father who returned back to reading his magazine. Her mother closed her eyes and fell asleep while her sister was looking at her school package excitedly.

"Can you imagine that, Alison? They have music classes at high school! That alone is so much better than our previous Japanese school!" Carrie exclaimed. "I hope I make new friends and enjoy a great time there!"

Yea, I sure hope I do. Alison turned away and a single drop of tear made its way down her pale cheeks.

****

The first thing Alison felt when she saw their new "home" was simply despair. It was better than what she had expected and the interior was relatively clean. But the moment she stepped into the house, she felt the faint musky scent of smog- a probable result of some chemical towers nearby. It was nothing like the faint woody smell she enjoyed inhaling in their old Machaya. However, everyone else was pretty excited- even her Dad- so it was probably just her bad mood getting the better of her.

"Sorry, are you the Goodall family? " A blonde man in his late forties poked his head into the house as the door was left open. Alison surveyed him curiously. She looked just like this American- appearance wise- and she felt uncomfortable of being surrounded by so many people of her own race after so long of seeing Asians everywhere.

"Yes, that's us." Her mother emerged from the kitchen and greeted the guest with a pleasant voice.

"I'm John and we're the Kingstons from next door and I just wanted to say hello to our new neighbours." The man smiled warmly and reached out to shake my mother's hand. Previously, in Japan, everyone would have bowed and exchanged polite yet mundane greetings. Alison felt a little funny doing the Western way.

"We're so honoured you paid a visit to our humble house," her mother chimed in her high-pitched voice. This was something she often said to their guests in Japan but somehow, it seemed overly formal here in America.

"Don't mention it, which school are your kids enrolled in?" He peered interestedly at Carrie and Alison.

"Cornwall Institution, a rather reputable school, I've heard," her father added easily. The truth was, Cornwall Institution was the only high school in Seattle which was prepared to accept Alison and her sister. Since they had no formal American education, they would lag behind their other peers and her parents were just thankful they were able to find a school. The reputation no longer mattered to them.

The man looked happy when he heard that. "It's such a coincidence but my kids are studying there. I've a son, Alex, who's sixteen and a younger daughter, Jane, who's fourteen," he answered cheerily.

"Jane's my age!" Carrie cried out. "Alison! This Alex person is of your age too! Maybe you would get to be in the same class!"

"Yea, sure," Alison mumbled and barely managed a weak smile. There was no way she would get acquainted with her neighbour's son. Imagine him knowing what you were like in school and at home. For her, it was way too close for comfort.

"Raising two kids surely takes a lot of effort," her mother said sincerely. "I can't imagine having any more!" She laughed and after some hesitation, Alison's father joined in.

"I have three actually. My eldest who's nineteen this year has just entered university and he's going to teach at Cornwall as a part-time job," John said proudly.

Hopefully, I'll never get to meet him – ever. Alison thought. At this moment, John interrupted loudly, "I don't suppose you have any transportation to school? For the children? The school is of a considerable distance from here."

For a moment there, her parents looked a little uncomfortable. They didn't want to tell this man that they couldn't afford private transportation and had decided to let Alison and Carrie take public transport there.

Seeing their sheepish expressions, John nodded. "I see. Would you mind if I drop your children alongside with mine? I'm sure it would be a real thrill for them to see kids of their own age every morning instead of their balding old dad."

Alison laughed loudly at his joke and her mother silenced her with a glare before bowing politely and said, "Thank you so much, Mr Kingston."

"We'll always be indebted to you," her father said respectfully.

"Yea, thanks so much, Mr Kingston!" Carrie gave him a toothy smile.

Hm, thanks so much. Alison thought sarcastically. Now, she was starting to dread school - even before it has started.

***

"Now, I want you to be as polite as possible, especially to Mr Kingston's kids," her mother instructed the sisters as they waited for John Kingston's black Volvo to turn around the driveway. Carrie, who was decked out in a white T-shirt and a Gap skirt, was bobbing up and now joyfully and she glanced at her watch from time to time- impatient for school to start.

Alison, on the other hand, was the complete opposite. She wore a hoodie (despite the hot weather) and dark blue jeans with a bag slung over her shoulders. She was wary as she peered at the road, half-heartedly hoping that Mr Kingston's car would break down.

At long last, the black Volvo stopped in front of them and the purring of the engine disturbed Alison's thoughts. Mr Kingston stuck his head and out and said, "You can hop on now!"

Carrie eagerly lunged forward to sit at the back while Alison lingered behind with her eyes darting back and forth. She briefly spotted a blonde-haired girl who was listening to music and a bespectacled fair-haired boy who was scribbling on his notebook.

"Alison? Are you getting on the car? " Mr Kingston was gazing at her with a strange look and Alison nodded silently before climbing into the front seat. She didn't feel comfortable squeezing with people at the back. Besides, she needed to prepare herself emotionally and mentally for the first day of school which can be rather torturing.

"Hey, Alison, what classes are you taking at Cornwall?" Mr Kingston asked as they zoomed past a grocery store. Alison carefully took out the schedule which came in the mail and frowned. "I'm taking English, English Literature, History and Earth Science," she answered dutifully.

At this moment, the fair-haired boy sitting at the back looked up. His interest seemed to be piqued, "Which homeroom are you in?"

"502."

"That's nice, you're in the same class as me," he said in a friendly tone. Alison stared at him for a few moments and shrugged. "I suppose so," she mumbled.

"I suppose this must be very different from Japan?" Mr Kingston asked. "I've always wanted to go to Asia but never had the chance."

"Well, Mr Kingston, I'm sure you wouldn't miss anything! America's so much more exciting than Japan!" Carrie cut in as she snuck a peek at Mr Kingston's daughter who was strenuously ignoring her.

Gritting through her teeth, Alison grumbled, "I think the East is much better than the West."

"You think so?" Mr Kingston laughed merrily. "Wait till you experience the American culture. I bet you won't even think about Japan anymore." He said it so confidently as if it was true.

No way. Alison pulled a face and sighed. Whether she liked it or not, there was no escaping from the fact that she would not be returning to Japan. Her only hope was to finish high school as soon as possible and apply for a Japanese college.

Not that her parents would ever approve of that. They wanted her to go Sarah Lawrence or even Washington State University but the point was, by then, she would be an adult so who would care?

Possibly no one.

Meeting

 ***

"Oh my gosh Megan, that hairstyle is so sweet!"

"Did you hear the latest rumour? Jessica is apparently in a relationship with Arthur!"

"Get real! Say, have you done the holiday homework? I need some back up."

The endless chattering in the corridors made Alison a little nervous. The moment she saw the large plaque declaring Cornwall's opening in 1956, her official enrolment in this school seemed to be more or less official. Even Carrie was a little shy. Her eyes were gazing in awe as she took in everything at once. Alison caught sight of some of the older girls' chic and trendy outfits and felt a little out of place and inferior.

If she had been in her old school, everyone would line up in a neat row without taking to each other the moment they entered the school compounds. It certainly wouldn't sound like a market place. Suddenly, she felt a poke at her shoulders. She looked up and found Alex smiling at her, unperturbed by her hostility.

Sighing, she asked wearily, "What do you want?"

"I just thought you would want to register yourself at the homeroom." He waved his student card casually and Alison nodded before following him. They slowly weaved through the large clusters of people and went past the Staffroom which had a "Forbidden: Enter at Your Own Risk" sign on the large imposing doors. A few teachers walked out of the door at that moment.

"Today's going to be a really busy day!" An old guy with a thinning hairline guffawed as he clutched his old mug filled with bitter coffee. Another woman in a red suit gazed at him sympathetically. At this moment, Alison spotted a man, no, a boy, who was lingering behind. He seemed too young to be a professor and yet, he had a teacher's pin on him. This was not to say he wasn't attractive. His messy blonde hair was brushed to the side and his face was smooth yet impassive. Decked out in a white polo shirt and low slung jeans, he would have fitted in better amidst the throngs of students rather than with the students. He looked up and caught Alison looking at him. She blushed and ran off instantly to catch up with Alex, almost embarrassed to be noticed by him.

"Hey, Alison! Here! " Alex waved at her and disappeared into one of the classrooms. She followed suit and found herself standing in front of a classroom filled with messily arranged chairs and clusters of noisy and boisterous people. Alison spotted the teacher in the red suit earlier and she walked up to her, flashing her card.

"Good morning, madam, I'm Alison Goodall, a new student here. Nice to meet you," she introduced herself and bowed lowly- just like what she did in Japan.

"Well, well, a student who finally has some decent manners." The woman seemed happy and she took down her name. "You can sit anywhere you like, so long as someone hasn't occupied the seat."

"Thank-you, Madam." Alison bowed again and saw some people whispering and pointing at her. Was her Japanese way of greeting people really strange? Shrugging off their comments, she took an isolated seat near the window while observing her soon-to-be classmates.

A bunch of girls donning low-cut dresses and heavy make-up was gathered in a corner. They pouted their lips and shared all the endless gossip they knew of. One of them with flame orange hair noticed Alison staring at them and she glared back at her. Alison shifted her gaze abruptly and pretended to be immersed in watching a fly crawl across her desk.

"Are you the new student?" A soft voice asked and Alison turned her head. A rather nerdy-looking girl with her messy black hair pulled back into a bun was looking at her. And she was sitting in the seat next to her. This meant that they were going to be partners for a full term.

"Yes, I am Alison Goodall," Alison said reluctantly. "That's nice. I'm Angela Brown, nice to meet you," she hugged her and Alison's eyes widened. She wasn't really used to such informal and intimate ways of greetings. Still, this Angela person seemed rather nice.

"Is it tough being here?" Alison asked curiously.

"Not really," Angela relaxed. "It's fine as long as you don't bear the wrath of the "Mean Girls" and the "Bad Boys" gang." She quoted the names with inverted commas.

"Who're they?" "Those over there," Angela pointed to the earlier bunch of aggressive looking girls and another group of boys on the opposite side of the room. Alison followed her gaze. She was quite sure she would be steering clear of them from now on.

"By the way, do you know Alex Kingston?" Alison asked conversationally.

Angela nodded. "I've hung out with him a few times. Do you like him?" Her face was wide-eyed with interest.

"What? No! " Alison muttered defensively. Was this how American teens react all the time? A simple question about a boy seemed to lead people thinking you might like the person in question. She had better be careful of what she said in this less than conservative society. "He's my neighbour," she explained.

"Well, he's a nice kid though. It's his sister who's the bad one."

"His sister? You don't mean, Jane Kingston?" Alison leant forward. "How can she be bad? I have seen the Kingston family and they're pretty nice and down to earth people."

"Well." Angela looked thoughtful. "This is strictly a rumour but I've heard of people saying she dabbles in drugs." She glanced around furtively and lowered her voice, "Also, her best friend is actually the head of the Mean Girls Gang. The one with the orange hair called Jessica."

"Wow." Angela mouthed and snuck another peek at the girl called Jessica who was now busy painting her nails. She never expected that such a respectable family like the Kingstons could produce a rebel like Jane. She had better made sure to stay away from her then. "This is so different from Japan, where I lived for a while," she added.

"I heard the Japanese are very conservative," Angela put in helpfully and Alison smiled for the first time-she was gradually warming up to her. "Yea, they're very tight lipped and not so rowdy as the Americans."

"You must wish to return to Japan." Angela saw Alison's wistful expression and reached out to squeeze her hand. "Don't worry, you'll love Seattle soon even though it's filled with some pretty silly people."

"Right," Alison questioned doubtfully. Why does everyone always say that?

***

The lessons flew past like the blur of the wind. And despite the fact that Alison was prompted to make an introduction at every class, she was nonetheless happy to have survived 3/4s of the day. During lunch break, she walked up to the cafeteria lady and got a serving of some disgusting meat and peas (her least favourite food).

"Alison! Over here! " Angela was waving at her and Alison gratefully made her way there. She was relieved that she would not have to suffer the embarrassment of sitting alone.

"I wish that they would one day make some edible food here," Alex groaned as he stuck a fork into the morose-looking piece of meat. Alison placed her tray down on the table and she sat next to him.

"That's why I pack my own lunch," Angela proclaimed proudly as she took out her lunchbox. There were green veggies, fish and rice in it. It strangely reminded Alison of how the Japanese ate.

"I wouldn't want to eat those healthy food. I think I'll stick to my dish." Alex shrugged and he eyed Alison eagerly. "So how's your first day of school?"

"Not bad," she answered truthfully and took a gulp of her Coke, letting the cool liquid slide down her parched throat.

"What do we have next?" A girl named Maggie (a good friend of Angela) who had a rather pudgy looking face asked.

"English." Angela instantly brightened up. "Anyway, isn't it cool we got the new and young teacher?"

"New and young?" Alex asked sceptically. "Since when? I thought all the teachers were at least in their mid-forties."

Alison snorted and Angela merely sighed. "I heard he's really handsome," she said wistfully. "And I heard his name is called Edward. Just imagine, what a cool name." Alison merely shrugged. She wasn't interested in boys in general and least of all, a hot young professor. It was probably all these American girls letting their raging hormones get the better of them. She didn't know what the appeal was but she found it silly that people actually lusted after a teacher.

Suddenly, she noticed Alex remain unmoving next to her. "Alex?" She waved a hand in front of him.

He blinked.

"Ang, did you just say the smoking hot teacher's name is called "Edward"?" He gulped, looking all nervous and scared like a kid who was caught steady candy in the sweets shop.

"Yea, why?" Angela's eyebrows rose. "Are you just jealous of him? Admit it, Alex, you're a pretty average-looking boy."

"No, I didn't mean that. What I meant was-"

"What do you mean Alex? Just spit it out." Maggie shot him a baleful look.

"Edward Kingston is my brother."

***

"I still can't believe Edward Kingston is your brother of all people," Angela repeated it for the third time, still seemingly unrelenting. She was gazing at Alex in awe, almost unwilling to believe that such different people – a Greek God and a normal mortal- shared DNA-similar genes.

"Get real," Alex muttered under his breath. He looked like he wanted to throw up.

"You must be proud of having such a high-achieving brother," Alison commented meaningfully, exchanging side looks with Angela.

"You'll see later. He's not well known for his pretty boy looks." Alex cringed as he got his books out of the locker and slapped the door back- real hard.

"What's he well known for then?"

"For being a maniac dictator like Hitler."

***

The classroom was silent and still for once. As the cliché old saying went, "It's so quiet that one can hear a pin drop". This saying fitted so perfectly for this scene. Nobody dared to swivel their eyeballs to the side, chat with their friends or pass secret notes to one another (a traditional American custom which Alison had learnt). In fact, the mood was so creepy that Alison wondered if she would actually prefer the previous unruly class.

She could hear Angela's pencil scrapping frantically against the paper and Alison turned her attention back to the paper Alex's brother, their new English teacher, had given out. While they were all slogging their guts out doing this quiz, Mr Edward Kingston was staring at his Macbook, oblivious to all the evil stares he was getting.

Alison finally believed what Alex had said of his brother. Although he was only nineteen, he seemed far too mature and in a perpetually bad mood all the time. The moment he stepped into class, he scolded everyone and gave the entire class detention for no apparent reason. After that, he then gave out a worksheet and threatened that whoever dared to utter even a syllable would have to stay back to "have a nice talk" with him. Personally, Alison knew that some girls from the MGG wouldn't mind. They all started flirting with him until he slammed his book down and startled all of them. Alex said that his brother had an uptight personality.

He probably just has some personal issues with everyone, even strangers.

Alison reluctantly turned back to the first question.

Who is William Shakespeare?

What kind of question was that? Thankfully, since she was an avid classic reader, she quickly scribbled down the answer.

Who is William Shakespeare's wife?

What? Who cares who his wife is? Was it Anne or Anna? Alison frowned and wrote down the latter.

"Mr Edward Kingston!" A loud voice came from the back.

Everyone stopped breathing- literally- and turned their heads to look at their saviour or in other words, the idiot who was brave enough to stand up to the monstrous teacher.

It turned out to be the head of the Bad Boys' Gang (BBG), one of the most rebellious kids in the school, a guy named a. His hair was gelled up to a side and those prominent freckles on his face made him look even uglier. Still, Alison was surprised that he had the guts to challenge Edward Kingston.

"Yes, Mr Albo?" Edward Kingston fixed a steely gaze on him.

Robert shrank back a little but straightened himself up and glared at the teacher. "Mr Kingston, aren't you only nineteen this year?"

"Yes."

"And we're all sixteen-year-olds this year."

"I assume your intelligence has allowed you to figure that out," Edward Kingston added dryly.

"Well, so you're older than us by three years... right?"

"In case you don't know, Mr Albo, middle school section is at another part of the school. If you're accidentally placed in the wrong class which looks to be more advanced than your level, please feel free to walk out of here." Edward Kingston smirked.

There was a pause.

And then one of the geeks clapped and shouted, "You did it, Mr Kingston!"

Alison spotted Edward Kingston's lips pull back into a triumphant smirk as Robert's legs gave way and he simply sank back in his seat. She had to grudgingly admit that he was really swift with his words and had the demeanour and authority to control even Robert, literally, the bully and terror of the school.

"Now, would anyone else want to challenge me like poor Mr Robert Albo over there?" Edward Kingston's eyes swept across the room and Alison froze when his gaze landed on her. His blue eyes bore into her and she flinched, wondering if she had broken any attire rules.

But within a split second, he moved on and simply waved his hand, "Carry on with your work."

"He's so frightening but so suave," Angela whispered to Alison.

"Suave, my foot," Alison mumbled back.

But for once, she had to agree with Angela.

On the frightening part of course.

First Encounter

"Alison? Can I speak to you?"

Alison was just about to leave the class when the the Terror (the new nickname which everyone gave him) called out to her. She paused, wondering if she had done anything wrong.

"What does he want?" she murmured.

"Don't know, it can't be anything good," Angela mumbled. She was utterly thrown off by the Terror's behaviour and she was finally convinced that Terror's good looks weren't enough to make up for all those loopholes in his personality.

"Imagine going out a date with him. He would probably lecture you on something. Not my ideal type."

That was what Angela had said and Alex fervently agreed with her- even though Edward Kingston was technically his blood brother.

"We'll meet you in Spanish." Angela nudged her and she left. Reluctantly, Alison turned her body towards the Terror and avoided looking at his blue eyes which seemed to mesmerize her all the time.

"Yesss, Mr Kingston?" Alison drew her words out. She was tired or weary and she only had one last period left before she had the chance to go home. And while she appreciated the importance of staying back and talking to the teacher, she kept eyeing the door and suppressing the desire to bolt out immediately.

"You're the new transfer student, am I right? The one who moved in next door to my family? " His face was emotionless now and Alison was suspicious. Why was he asking all these now?

"I expect someone of your calibre would figure that out a long time ago. I'm friends with your brother, Alex," she said, not bothering to be polite at all. She figured that the only way to deal with such people was to do it through the rude way. The unpleasant thought came to her that she was suddenly becoming less Japanese than she had liked to and more American.

"And so it seems. You seem mature for your age, Alison."

"Did you ask me to stay back to talk all these?" Alison frowned. This was a complete waste of time and she turned to go.

"No, wait!" He grabbed her arm and she took a step back, as if she was jolted by electricity. Edward Kingston quickly withdrew his hand and his gaze softened, "I just hope that you would enjoy your experience here."

"I would enjoy it if you would let me to, Mr Kingston! " Alison huffed and barged out of the classroom.

Who did he think he was? Just because he was Mr Kingston's son and a senior didn't meant that he could use his authority to boss everyone around. It was just a shame that he was bestowed with such good looks. Life wasn't fair after all.

Then again, since when was life fair? She had wanted to opt for Japanese as a 2nd language but they didn't offer that as a core. Now, she was forced to take up Spanish, a language she had no remote contact with previously. How was she supposed to catch up?

Whether she wanted to or not, she was just going to blame Edward Kingston for all the bad things today and although she felt the tiniest bit guilty, pleasure swelled within her.

He deserved it after all.

He was a jerk.He's such a disgusting, foul, irrit-

Alison stopped. She took a quick look at the place card on the classroom door and feeling slightly puzzled, she stuck her head in to check if this was her class. Angela had saved her a seat and she was trying to catch my attention.But... but...

"Miss Goodall? You may come in." An all-too-familiar voice sounded out.

For the second time in the day.

"Why is Edward Kingston teaching me bloody Spanish?"

Oops, she had said that out loud.

******

"Miss Goodall, do you realize what your mistake is? " Principal Audrey asked as she smoothed the creases on her immaculate Christian Dior suit.

"Yes, I am humbly aware of my wrongdoings," Alison whispered- the same thing she had always said and practiced in Japan. Her eyes surveyed the air-conditioned Principal's room. It was filled with plaques and newspaper cuttings of Cornwall Institution and there was a huge pile of reference books in a bookshelf. Not an ideal place where she wanted to spend her afternoon.

She didn't want to say this. But it was not even her fault that she had actually said a rude, demeaning word in front of the teacher. It hadn't even occurred to her that she had said it out loud. But she knew she did when snickers started erupting from the students and there was an amused smile on the Terror's face.

Relieved that the Terror wasn't bursting with anger, Alison hurried to her seat but not before that cold, rough voice said, "You're sent to detention, Miss Goodall."

Oh hell.

Returning back to the present, she could only sigh and blankly stared at her hands, wondering if her parents would ground her for getting trouble on the first day of school. She was devoid of anger or any emotion because she was trained not to show any signs of weakness in front of others.

"Are you all right, Miss Goodall? Apart from this…small incident, I'm assuming you are fitting well in school? " Principal Audrey put on a sympathetic voice, as if she felt pity for her. Alison felt anger brew in her chest. She didn't want sympathy or pity. If she hadn't been taught to be courteous, she would have just banged the table or do something drastic just like Robert.

"Yes.. I'm fine, Madam," she said hesitantly in a controlled, strained voice. "May…may I go now?"

"Yes, you may, I'll speak to Mr Kingston about this incident. I trust you wouldn't repeat the same offence again."

Whatever. Alison wanted to say but she merely nodded and bolted out of that terrifying office. The school was silent- having emptied of all the students around an hour earlier. Grinding some silver coins in her hand against one another, Alison was about to head towards the bus stop to take public transport before a loud voice shouted out, "Alison!"

She stopped.

She couldn't believe it.

It was bloody Terror.

Swivelling her head mechanically around like a robot, Alison saw him leaning against the car alongside with Alex, Jane and Carrie.

Alex's face lightened up when he saw her, "Alison! Over here! " He waved and Alison raised her hand weakly before making her way slowly there.

"What took you so long? " Carrie demanded and Alison mumbled, "Er, I had a talk with Principal Greene. Why did you wait for me? "

If Carrie hadn't not been confused already, she was by that point. Scratching her head, she said vaguely, "Well, Edward said we had to wait."

"Yea, he should. After all, he was the one who got you into all that trouble," Alex muttered darkly. The Terror, who had remained silent up to this moment, merely shrugged and got into the car. He had changed out of his office uniform and wore a dark green T-shirt and jeans. In fact, he looked really nice.

Alison shook off that thought and climbed into the car. "Buckle your seat belts, kids," he advised and Alison could hear Alex mutter, "Back off." Alex seemed to display a lot of resentment towards his brother.

Nodding woodenly, she pulled out her journal and peered at the list of must-do things. She wouldn't have any free time today. Her exasperated sigh caught the Terror's attention.

"Homework?" The musical voice of Edward Kingston was hard to resist but Alison stealthily ignored him- much to his chagrin.

"Seriously, brother, why do you have to get a job at Cornwall of all places? " Alex's angry voice blared out in the background.

"Oh please, Alex, what's it with you? I'm just so happy Edward worked at our school. " The high-pitched voice of Jane Kingston was prominent. "All my friends just idolize him and I've upped my popularity points by telling everyone that he's related to me." She sounded smug.

Alison turned her head to look at the young girl. She was pretty but she gave off a hostile vibe similar to the MGG. Angela was right, as usual. This girl meant trouble and clearly, she adored her eldest brother unlike Alex.

"I was hoping you haven't been doing that. I've received a few confession notes today." Edward Kingston laughed and Alison looked up in surprise. Strangely, the Terror seemed more....humane and normal when he wasn't working as a teacher. Maybe the oppressing education system at Cornwall was accountable for his earlier bad attitude.

Noticing her gaze, Edward's eyes shifted to her. "You lived in Japan for awhile?" he asked.

"Yes."

"Is it any better than America?"

"Yes."

Alison stared rigidly at the windscreen as she awkwardly sat next to her teacher. Still, Edward Kingston was more of a senior and she was still struck by how striking his face was and that he always seemed to be deep in thought. Also, there's that smallest issue of him being her neighbour. Not that that would bother her of course. She wouldn't go to all that trouble to worry about such a trivial issue.

"Hey, Alison, can I go to your house later to do the homework," Alex piped up. "Huh? Why?" She was surprised. Why would anyone walk barely three feet to another place to do his work? But when she saw the glum look on his face, she instantly understood. He wanted to escape from the ominous presence of his brother. If she had a sibling like that, she would have fled a long time ago.

"Sure, Alex, you can," Alison smiled. Evidently, she was friendlier to him now because he was actually a rather nice person although she still hadn't gotten the chance to ask him about his involvement in the BBG. Maybe some other day.

"Can I come over then?" Edward Kingston asked, a small smile playing on his lips.

Alison gulped and turned away. "Look, brother, I'm sixteen and I don't need some looking after! Go away, please," Alex retorted from behind.

"I was just curious on how Alison's house looked like."

"Get real, if I didn't know better, I would think you're interested in her which can't be true," Alex spat out viciously. "Because you have a girlfriend!"

Alison froze. He had a girlfriend? Of course he would have someone. He's just too attractive for the general public. Somehow, her heart was beating so fast she almost felt like fainting.

"I didn't know you had one," Alison said, deadpan.

"Well, fine, he used to have one. Her name's Amber and she met him at th-" Alex rambled on and Edward Kingston silenced him with a piercing look. He was reverted back to his Terror self.

"If you say one more work, Alex Kingston, I'll kill you. Believe me," his voice was dangerously soft.

Alex scowled and caught Alison's eye in the rear view mirror.

"See what I told you?" he mouthed conspicuously. Alison nodded. All her suspicions and fears were confirmed. Edward Kingston was truly a jerk.

So why did she care that he used to have a girlfriend?

*****

The moment she reached home, Alison put her bag neatly by her study table while Carrie threw hers on the floor. "I'm so beat," she groaned, flinging herself onto her makeshift bed.

"How was your day? You were pretty quiet during the car journey." Alison started pulling her journals and worksheets out. Turning around, she saw that Carrie was sullen, unlike her normal chatty self.

"Are you alright?" Alison started but Carrie shook her head. "I'm fine. It just hasn't been a good day for me."

"Why?" Alison wasn't exactly morbidly curious.

"None of your business." Her sister's tone was a tad too sharp.

"Fine, whatever." She put up her hands defensively and left the room. She hated messing around with other people businesses but sometimes she was forced to because these were people she cared for and loved.

"Alison! Alison! " Her mother's soft voice pulsed through her thoughts.

"Yes, Mother?" She went out to the living room and stopped short. Both Alex and Edward Kingston were standing there and she wasn't really happy about seeing one of them in particular. The tall, dark handsome one.

"What are you doing here? You aren't invited here. " She darted him an aggressive, complacent look. Her mother drew in a sharp rasp of breath. "Alison! Where are your manners? Mr Kingston is your teacher! He's just here to help his brother and your schoolwork. I'm just so pleased to have him here." Her mother scolded her lightly and gave a faux smile to the Terror who returned a polite grin in return.

"I'm sure Alison has her own views. Of course, I will leave if she doesn't want me to be here." He was pretending to be a gentleman in front of the adults. That was one of his tricks.

"Of course, I'll have none of that! " Alison's mother clapped her hands together in unison. "Just take a seat, Mr Kingston and may I just say, I'm wholly impressed by your credentials." She beamed, visibly impressed.

"Thanks for your compliments, Mrs Goodall." Edward Kingston looked pleased yet modest at the same time. Alex muttered, "Show-off" and went to sit on the sofa, looking all depressed and ill.

"I'll... just get the drinks," she mumbled and shot into the kitchen. Alex followed her and he leant against the table top with his arms folded across his chest.

"So, it's tough on you, having such a brother," Alison started as she laid out the glasses and took out a few cans of Coke from the refrigerator.

"Tough? More like horrendous." Alex stuck his tongue out and moaned, "He's such a know-it-all and too bloody perfect. I can't even match up to him. "

"You aren't jealous of him, aren't you?" Alison said in a half-teasing tone.

"Me? Jealous? Okay, maybe you're alright. I hate it when Dad and Mum compare me to him." He grudgingly admitted as he helped himself to some sweets in the candy jar.

"An over-achiever?"

"Straight-As student. You know he got into Stanford as an early admission? " Alison could hear him sucking on the pile of chewing gum and she cautiously asked, "Well, you know about that girlfriend of his, who is she? I mean, I'm not interested in his life or anything. Just curious. "

"What?" Alex looked up, slightly surprised at her approach to this sudden topic. "Oh, Amber? She was an honours student who used to study in Cornwall as well. They're of the same age. She was literally the belle of the school before she left." He drew the word "belle" out so that she could get his point.

"And I reckon the Terror was the beau?"

"You gotcha." Alex unwrapped another sweet and popped it into his mouth. "I'm not that close to him but I can tell he has issues. Personal ones."

"Really?" Alison's voice went higher than usual and taking a steadying breath, she calmly said, "He looks like he has virtually everything."

"He's so complicated, no one understands him." Alex winced and looked contemplative. " But in my opinion, what he lacks is love. Real love," he added when he spotted Alison's sceptical face. "I personally think Amber's just a high-school crush or a fling."

Turning away, Alison blushed as a faint pink tinged her cheeks. What was she doing? Asking about so much info on Edward Kingston? It gives people the wrong impression that she was remotely interested in him when obviously, it's not the case.

"You know, Alex, you're an extremely perspectival person," Alison observed.

"Welcome to the club." He snorted and walked out of the kitchen and then, he turned around again.

"By the way, my brother doesn't drink Coke. He drinks organic juices." He pronounced it in disgust- as if it was the name of a plague or a disease.

Sigh. I was hoping you wouldn't say that. Alison grabbed the tray and strode straight out of the kitchen.

***

Deep Understanding

By the time one week had passed, Alison felt more confident to deal with school. With her newly finished homework in her bag, she grabbed a copy of Pride and Prejudice and stumbled her way to the main door after finishing a hastily-made egg mayo sandwich.

Opening the door, she found Alex waiting outside patiently. It was a routine now. She would hitch a ride with Mr Kingston and talk to Alex on the way. Her new best friend instantly grinned when he saw her and waved. "Great day today. Where's your sister"

"She'll be down soon." Alison shrugged. Carrie had been behaving strangely lately. She seemed more depressed and morose and she was staying out later and later as every night went past. Her parents didn't suspect that anything was amiss because her sister was a naturally responsible person. Still, she couldn't help feeling that something was just not right. Alison flipped open her cell phone. 0 missed messages. It wasn't as if she had any friends to send private messages too. She followed Alex and took a lift down together before disccusing whether their newly arrived German neighbour was possibly an alien.

Jane was already waiting downstairs and she was wearing a low-cut V-shaped shirt with a short skirt. She glanced distastefully at them and turned away to continue yapping to some friend on her cell phone.

"Is your sister's outfit actually legal? " Alison nodded disapprovingly towards the petite figure. Alex grimaced. "It isn't. But nobody really cares at Cornwall. Besides, my parents think she's just going through a teenage phase."

"Do you know she's part of the Mean Girls Gang?" Alison asked, her eyes still on the scantily clad girl.

"Huh? What do you mean?" Alex scratched his head. He had a puzzled and blank look on his face.

"Never mind," Alison said with a wave of her hand. Feeling slightly guilty, she turned away. She had wanted to ask Alex about his sister's involvement with those girls but decided against it. She didn't want to be responsible for any family breakups or rifts. Instead, she chose to listen to his endless talk on how he was positive that one of the school cleaners was a witch from Mars.

*****

"I'm handing out your latest Spanish quiz." Edward Kingston announced as he took out a stack of worksheets from the drawer.

"Alice Johnston."

"Anna Winster."

"Alex Kingston."

Alex went up and took the paper without even looking at his brother. He was still embarrassed about having a sibling as a teacher.

"How did you do? " Angela nudged him.

"Angela Weber."

Once Angela went up to the front of the class, Alex pouted. "You know, considering the fact that I'm his brother. He could have been more partial towards me."

"That's favouritism," Alison pointed out.

"Still, it's a nice dream."

"Alison Goodall."

At this junction, Alison could feel her muscles and tendons stiffen and she grudgingly went up to collect her paper.

"Look for me after class," he muttered by her ear and she nodded. She had taken a peek at her paper and knew what he was going to say. She returned back to her seat.

"That bad, huh?" Angela frowned. "But he can't blame you. Everyone else here has half a year ahead of you."

"Thanks for telling me that."

"Hey, don't fret, look, I had half a year ahead and we still got the same score," Alex put in helpfully.

Alison fixed his attention on her paper. "That really helps, you know," she said slowly.

"Sorry." Alex rolled his eyes.

For the rest of the period, it merely flew past in a blur. When the bell rang, signalling the ending of the class, Alison went up to the Terror and braced herself for her lecture.

"Look, Alison, I'm not going to scold you." His face softened when he saw her. "I'm aware you haven't taken Spanish at all for your entire life. Principal Audrey told me that you're fluent in Japanese?"

"Yes." What was he trying to hint at?

"Well." A smile threatened, either in triumph or happiness, and Edward Kingston nodded. "I've made special arrangements. I'll give you private tuition in Spanish every day after class until you achieve a certain level of proficiency."

"Wha-what?" Alison staggered back as she searched his face for any sign of humour. But he looked dark and serious. He wasn't kidding at all.

"But, Mr Kingston, I-"

"No objections are to be made. In return, you're to teach me Japanese." A playful smirk lingered on the edges of his lips.

"Look, Mr Kingston, I...I can't do that. I mean, I can just learn from Alex or something and besides, you don't require a use of Japanese either." Alison hurriedly came up with any excuse she could think of.

"Firstly, since Alex is my brother, I can comment on his proficiency at Spanish which is rather... not very excellent, as one might say." He flashed his brilliant set of teeth. "And secondly, I'm planning to major in mass communications or public relations in university so I'm sure I need another language when handling Japanese clients."

"How many languages do you actually know, Mr Kingston?" There was a sarcastic edge to her tone.

"Oh, just like everyone else," he said carelessly. "I only know German, Mandarin, Italian and Korean for a start."

Alison shook her head slowly in anger. It was no use arguing with this infuriating man, no, boy, because he could come up with a witty comment for just about everything.

"But-" she protested, feeling slightly harassed.

"That's the end of your questioning. Consider it a gift."

Seeing that he wasn't going to cave in to her demands, she simply said, "Thank you, sir", grabbed both her paper and bag, and left.

Upon hitting the corridors this time, Alison merely took her time to walk to her next class. She needed time to think and rid her mind of any angry thoughts directed at a certain someone. She just hoped to be left alone and tossed a coin before inserting it into the drinks vending machine.

"Goodbye suckers, let's hit the nail bar, girls! " Some tittering and chattering from around the corner made Alison look up in amazement.

Alison's eyes widened. She recognized that voice anywhere. It was Carrie; it surprised her when she saw her sister with the Mean Girls Gang. Not just that, Jane Kingston was holding her by the arms as if they were best buddies. Carrie looked a lot different than when she saw her this morning. There was some pinks streaks in her hair, probably a result of dabbling with cheap hair dye, and there was a fake tattoo on her arm.

They turned around the corner and Carrie's eyes instantly met hers. She looked like she was jolted by fire and she casted her eyes down- ashamed and embarrassed.

Alison put up her hand and demanded, "What're you doing with my sister?"

Jessica, her hair now auburn red, sneered, "Sister? What sister? Just because you're not cool enough to join our team doesn't mean that someone else can't. Right, sistah? " She nudged Carrie to respond.

Alison was hurt. "Carrie, what are you doing? Return back to class now. " She tried dragging her away but someone- Jane most probably- broke her grasp.

"Watch it, know-it-all. Just because both my brothers like you doesn't mean that I adore you," Jane hissed as she stood in front of Carrie- as if she was protecting Carrie from her very own sister.

"Back off Jessica." Alison's face hardened as she squeeze the Can coke tightly. "My sister has her priorities on school work and I hope you would leave her alone."

"Oh really? If I had a bossy sister like you, I would have been put off." Jessica threw her an evil smile. Everyone in her gang laughed appreciatively.

"Carrie, say something! What are you doing with them?!"

"Shut up, Ali. It's none of your business. And if you dare tell Mum and Dad about this, I'm going to break off any ties with you," Carrie snarled and pursed her lips, taking a huge amount of effort to avoid her eye.

"But Carrie-" Alison's eyes brimmed with tears.

"C'mon girls, let's go funking and leave this moron behind," Jessica screeched and her gang clapped heartily. Carrie was hustled to the middle and the entire group left with Alison being alone in the hallway.

"Carrie! Carrie!" she screamed. "Come back here!" She dropped the Coke and the contents spilled everywhere but she was oblivious to it now.

There was no reply.

Carrie was gone.

******

She had no choice, no choice at all. Alison could only force herself to sit through the next couple of classes like a dead zombie. Angela and Alex were concerned but she merely said she felt a little ill. She couldn't believe it, that her sister was so gullible to fall for Jessica's or Jane's tricks and she simply couldn't accept the fact that her good-natured sister was led astray.

"Hey, Alison, are you sure you are okay? " Angela asked for the third consecutive time. She slid her eyes worriedly to her friend and touched Alison's shoulder. "You're not PMSing right?"

"Maybe I am," she answered curtly and looked down at her hands, annoyed that herself. If only she had paid more attention and recommended some decent friends for Carrie, her sister wouldn't feel the need to join the MGG.

"Angela?" she paused. "How bad are the people in the MGG?"

Angela opened her mouth to answer but clamped it shut again. She gave her a dubious look before saying, "Why do you want to know?"

"Just say it."

Noticing Alison's crestfallen expression, Angela nervously muttered, "Well, MGG is not as terrible as those violent street gangs. I mean, they're filled with normal school girls like us but well...." She ran her fingers through her hair and struggled to keep her gaze on Alison. "It's just that... I once heard... that Jessica does lure some of the girls to go....have...erm..intimate relationships with some guys."

Alison stared back at her, horrified. "Explain."

Angela looked away, clearly self-conscious as she bit her soft lips. "Look, I'm probably not the best person to tell you this. But...I do know some girls take drugs and when they're on high, they...tend to do stuff and go overboard at parties."

"Parties?" Alex overheard their conversation and leant forward to join in. "What are you guys talking about?"

"The Mean Girls Gang..."

"Oh right, Alison mentioned them once. Why are you guys talking about them?" Alex asked as he pulled a face at their Psychology teacher, a mousy woman called Mrs Prat.

"Alison wanted to know..." Angela caught sight of Alison's frozen expression and shrugged. "...about certain things." Angela noticed how her best friend's fingers drummed on the table top and how Alison seemed almost in a frenzy and too nervous. She acting all strange of a sudden.

Frowning, Alison asked, "Where do they usually host these parties?"

"Jessica's parents are rich and they practically give her almost a thousand pounds per month solely for entertainment." Angela looked disgusted. "Jessica always invites all her gang members and boys from the nearby Karin Boys School."

"Wow, how do you know all these?" Alex was clearly impressed and gave her an admiring look.

"I don't just live for video games like you. I do keep in touch with the schools' happenings." Angela rapped her knuckles, inviting Alex's wrath. "Alison, you okay?" she asked a split second later.

"I'm fine," Alison said weakly. She was torn between spilling out all her sorrows and just keeping mum before she could ask her too many questions that she didn't want to answer. Angela wrinkled her nose with disbelief, as if she didn't believe Alison's statement but she gave up and turned back to the writing assignment they were supposed to concentrate on. Alex returned to talking about the latest game, Battleship Star, with his partner, one of the geeks.

Though Alison couldn't put her finger on why Carrie acted in this way, she realized that there had always been signs. She certainly didn't change drastically overnight- it was a built up of supressed feelings from before. Back in Japan, she frequently expressed her hatred for the school she was in (Minaka Junior) and how she detested the formality of Japanese education, how reserved her classmates were and how some people avoided her because she was different. That was why she wanted to escape to America because she wanted to be with people she was similar to. It hadn't occurred to her that Carrie would be so silly as to fall for Jessica's trick and join the MGG just to be popular and accepted by people. Curses. Alison felt like slapping herself. She should have paid more attention to Carrie instead of worrying about herself. She was such a selfish person.

"So, um, Alison, do you want to go with us to shop for some books after school? " Angela stuttered.

After musing over it, she shook her head. "I'll pass. I-" Shit. Come up with some excuse so she wouldn't suspect anything. "I actually have extra Spanish class with Mr Kingston today," she finished.

"You're having extra classes with my brother of all people?" Alex stopped short. Clearly, his brother didn't seem to be the happiest topic for him and he didn't look enthused about the idea of her spending extra time with Edward Kingston. Sighing, Alison explained, "He insisted. He said I needed it."

"Just so typical." Alex raised an eyebrow and Angela gave her a meaningful look which she couldn't understand. She waited until Alex turned away before whispering to Alison, "Spit it out. Is the cause for your unhappiness because of Mr Edward Kingston?"

"Who gave you that idea?"

"I have seen how Edward Kingston looks at you in class when you aren't looking. I'm quite sure he likes you," she murmured.

"Angela!" Alison's mouth formed an O-shape. "He's a teacher, for goodness sake!"

"A rather hot one, don't you think?" Angela grinned cheekily. "Besides, he's only nineteen and your neighbour, I might add. You have plenty of chances to get close to him."

"That is the worse reason I've ever heard of for courting a guy."

"Sheesh, I know Edward Kingston's not my type after that horrendous class of his but if he's yours, I'll encourage you to go for it." She winked suggestively. Alison never knew Angela had this perverse side to her usually bubbly personality.

"You do know that in Japan, we'll never do these kind of things. Everything is supposed to be secret and discreet," Alison replied sorely.

"But Angela-"

"Yes?"

"Edward Kingston's a hot-blooded American teenager. You must do it the American way if you want to pursue him."

"And what's the American way?" Alison hissed.

"Go direct and straightforward. And never ever, look back," Angela answered triumphantly.

***

Falling in Love

Take Note: I haven't gotten the transition from mutual dislike to love for Edward and Alison exactly right so the flow seems a bit awkward for that part. Will edit after Nanowrimo. There might also be some errors in the timing because I changed parts of it For any other mistakes, please inform me via the comments section.

***

Although Alison wanted to throw a sickie (and Angela offered to cover up for her), she knew that it was better that she got this Spanish lesson over and done with.

Knock. Knock.

"Yes?" A soft musical voice sounded out and Alison frowned, all hopes of the Terror having left already dashed. "Erm, Mr Kingston?" she called out tentatively.

The door flew open instantly and Alison blinked. Edward Kingston had changed into a new blue shirt and jeans and she was just as awestruck by his appearance as she had the first time she saw him outside of school. "I thought you wouldn't come." Relief flooded his voice.

Alison stared ahead coldly and trudged into the room. To her surprise, she found Jessica, of all people, sitting at one desk. "What is she doing here?" Alison growled and jabbed a finger in her direction.

"She came up to me and wanted some Spanish tuition as well when she heard that I had offered an extra class for you," Edward Kingston smoothly said.

Alison's eyes narrowed and she took a seat, the one furthest away from that foul stinking girl. She still couldn't forget Carrie's betrayal and her negligence and seeing that girl so near her, she just wanted to pull her stinking blonde hair out.

Hang on. Was she acting too American? Alison shook of that thought. It was not possible. She had lived in Japan for 12 years. How can she act like an American within such a short span of time?

"So firstly, we've moved on from the alphabets and numbers, so I hope we can start with basic greetings." Edward Kingston's eyes were on both of them and Jessica leant forward eagerly, as if she wanted to devour him. It's no surprise to Alison. Obviously she would want to hook up with one of Cornwall's most eligible beaus. Too bad, he's taken. She realized this with a stinging sensation in her chest. Again, she questioned herself: Why did she care about that anyway?

He handed out a worksheet with basic vocabulary in them and Alison read it uninterestedly.

"So, we will move on to conversing using these basic sentences? Would you like to do it with each other or..." He paused.

Alison snarled and turned her head towards Jessica, as if daring her to actually come over and engage her in a polite conversation using Spanish. She didn't know any Spanish words or expletives but she sure know some Japanese and of course, English, swear words which wasn't going to be entirely pleasant from her.

"No thanks, Edward." Jessica flicked a strand of hair and said huskily, "I would prefer if we can do it with you individualyl. " Her eyes drew a line from him to her short and revealing shirt. Edward Kingston had the grace to actually look uncomfortable. "So, we would start with-" he began and turned to Alison with a hopeful look.

"No, me, me!" Jessica said in a shrill voice. Alison shrugged and nodded understandingly. She wasn't interested in doing this conversation thing herself and she could tell Jessica was dying to lay her hands on him. Might as well let her have the chance. Edward Kingston looked pained as he shifted his chair over to Jessica's seat. Well, serve him right. She thought.

Folding her arms around her, the sudden buzzing of the phone distracted her attention. "Hello?" Alison picked it up. "Alison, have you seen your sister?" It was her father. Alison felt her body stiffen and she whispered, "No Father, I haven't seen her today." She frowned. She hated telling lies to people- especially to her parents- and she knew what the consequences were.

"Where are you now?" Her father's cold, authoritative voice made her flinch. "I'm in school, having extra Spanish class with Mr Edward Kingston."

"Ah, that smart chap, eh?" "Yes."

"Fine, that's a reasonable excuse. Be sure to come home for dinner."

"Yes, Father."

"Goodbye."

"Goodbye, Father."

Alison breathed and clasped her cell phone cover shut. She noticed Edward Kingston staring at her and she turned away to hide her embarrassed face. Carrie hadn't returned home yet and she usually wasn't this late without even informing her parents. She needed to confront Jessica about this after the lesson.

Sighing, she suddenly had this prickly feeling of someone watching her. Lifting her head up, she saw Edward Kingston's eyes fixed in her direction, utterly oblivious as Jessica placed her hands onto his shoulder. Alison gulped and tried to break off from that stare but it was impossible to be oblivious to whatever was happening on the other side of the room.

"So, Mr Kingston, do you happen to have a girlfriend?" Jessica purred softly by his ears but it was loud enough to be heard anyway.

Alison pursed her lips. She couldn't pretend to be disinterested in whatever Edward Kingston had to say to Jessica. But there was the nagging feeling that reminded her that Edward Kingston was her teacher no less and it was wholly inappropriate to see Jessica having her hands all over him.

She observed Edward Kingston wince as he tried to pull away. "Please, Miss Harrow, a little decency..." But obviously this tactic wouldn't work on the Queen Bee of the school.

"Tell me, Edward, is it true that you were Prom King for your year?" Jessica continued her sultry act as she impatiently stroked his messy blonde hair. Alison felt sick as she witnessed this scene. One shouldn't mess around with a person of a higher ranking. That's what she learnt in Japan. But no, apparently, Jessica Harrow hasn't heard of the word "decency" before in her life. Or if she had, she certainly wasn't displaying it.

"Yes, if you will excuse me." Edward Kingston muttered irritably as he pulled her clingly, thin arm away as if it was a parasite. Alison wanted to laugh. It was almost impossible to fend off Jessica's amorous and lecherous advances.

"Oh, Edward, you know you want me," she cooed. At this point, Edward Kingston, seemingly exasperated and tired, merely retorted, "Can you get the fuck away? And by the way, I don't like blondes. I prefer brunettes." And strangely, he gave Alison a pointed look when he made that proclamation.

Drawing back, Jessica finally got the hint and her smooth (probably Botoxed) forehead crinkled with puzzlement. "What? You don't want me?" She was in a state of disbelief. As the Queen Bee, nobody dared to disobey her and certainly, she has always been able to obtain any boy she liked. It confused her to see Edward Kingston resist her flirty charms.

"Yes, and if you don't get my obvious hint, I suggest you go for an IQ test." Clearly, Jessica Harrow had tested the limits of his patience. It certainly wasn't unusual for Edward Kingston to be so rude.

"Well, fine, you'll pay heavily for resisting me," she snarled, baring her teeth before grabbing her hot pink Glitter bag and bolting out of the classroom.

"Wait-" Alison stood up quickly, wanting to run after her but Edward Kingston grabbed her arm. "No, Alison, you stay," he said firmly.

"Go away," she tried breaking from his grasp but to no avail. He didn't understand the severity of the situation. She wanted to question, no, threaten Jessica to stay away from her sister but she couldn't possible tell Edward Kingston that. He would blab to her parents and Carrie would get into deep trouble. Simply because of her.

"Stop this erratic behavior." He pulled her closer to him. Alison gazed into empty space. The feline figure had disappeared and she felt a sudden wave of despair.

"It's all your damn fault," Alison accused him aggressively.

"I was trying to prevent a fight from breaking out."

"I hate you," she spat, all emotions overwhelming her now. Edward Kingston's face changed into a picture of hurt and sorrow, as if her words truly affected him. Well, he should. Everything's his fault. If only she hadn't moved to this dreary old town. If only she had stayed in Japan and enjoy a peaceful quiet life. If only… If only….

"Alison, calm down." She hated him but his voice had a hypnotic effect to it. She sat down and held her arms tightly around her legs, like a vulnerable child. She hated showing this weak side to other people, in particular Edward Kingston, and she wondered if he would think that she was just a sore whiny loser. And as much as she didn't like to, she cared about what other people thought of her- even people whom she hates. Call it low self-esteem, but she still hasn't been able to completely escape from this part of her personality yet: the extreme self-consciousness of how people perceived her.

"YOU WANT ME TO CALM DOWN? DO YOU KNOW CARRIE MISSING? HOW DO YOU WANT ME TO STAY COOL AND COLLECTED?" she shouted.

"Hang on, your sister is missing?" Something clicked in his brain and he instantly understood why she was acting in such a delusional way.

"She's on drugs, at some party, oh, I don't know," Alison screamed, a little hysterical. It was all her fault. It always was. No wonder her parents blamed her all the time.

"Hush," he reached out his hands to wrap around her and she didn't resist. It felt so nice to be hugged by someone. She had never been hugged by her parents before and this was very comforting.

"What happened to her?" His steady voice eased her pain slightly. Alison didn't know the reason, but she felt safe and secure in his arms. The barriers between the teacher and the student soon faded away with his touch. It wasn't Mr Edward Kingston, her English teacher, whose arms were around her. It was just Edward Kingston, the 19-year-old teenage heartthrob from next door.

"She....I....I saw her with Jessica's gang, the MGG," she sobbed before hastily adding, "The Mean Girls Gang, if you don't understand what I meant."

He looked thoughtful for a second and his face instantly hardened. "I know what that gang is. It has a long history in our school."

"Huh?" Alison pulled away at last and stared at him.

He stared back, his blue eyes locked on hers. They were both silent and still, just gazing at each other. After a few seconds, Alison felt a weird flip in his stomach, a gnawing intuition that this was too strange, too intimate. As if he could see more of her than he should.

His face was dead straight and she surveyed his smooth forehead, the tiny lines around his eyes.

Clearing her throat, she broke the spell and turn away. She nervously fingered the hems of her skirt and Edward Kingston stepped forward.

"Alison, have you ever had someone confess to you before? " he murmured.

Alison felt a bit thrown. She was not used to this kind of focused attention. "I...no..." her face was drained with color, wondering why she was discussing her love life with him instead of coming up with a solution to find Carrie. "I was never that attractive to people of the opposite sex."

"How clueless you are." There was a glint in his eye and his tone was oblique. Alison felt a little flustered under his gaze. Her heart started beating more quickly and everything seems so heightened. She was aware of every single movement she made.

"Well, they...they always say that about me," Alison stuttered, trying to meet his deadpan expression, trying to ignore the fact that heat was rushing to her face, that the hairs pricking at the back, that she was uncomfortable with the way how his eyes bore into her, as if he wanted her to say something to him. Alison felt twinges all over the place and closed her eyes. She didn't know how he ever thought Edward Kingston wasn't good-looking. She must have been a little blind then.

"Alison?" he said softly and she could feel his warm breath on her dry skin.

"Yes?" she could barely speak.

"Is there any strict Japanese custom for kissing? I've heard how rigid you are about the Japanese ways," he asked breathlessly.

"No." Alison still didn't open her eyes. "I...I think they kiss pretty much the same way around the globe." What was he trying to drive at?

"Ah, I see." He sounded amused.

"Why did you ask?"

There was a pause and Alison felt a little frightened.

"So, I can do this."

He leant forward and Alison instantly felt his lips pressed gently against hers. Edward wrapped his arms around her and pulled her tighter to him. He's...Alison didn't know what to say. It was her first kiss but it was surprisingly enjoyable. He's so good. She explored his mouth with hers, inhaling that sweet scent of him, wondering how long this was going to go on. She wanted it to last forever and ever.

And then it hit her.He's your teacher. Your sister's still missing. She pulled away and as much as she felt terrible for doing it, she had to.He didn't answer, lifted his face and gazed at her. "You don't want to carry on doing this?" There were faint remnants of hurt and rejection in his voice and Alison couldn't bring herself to look at him.

"No.. it's just that, I think it's happening a little too fast for me. I... I need to go home and sort out my thoughts," she babbled.

"I see." He was silent and he jammed his hands into his pockets. He meets her eyes briefly and looks away again. Alison felt her chest tighten.

"So...can I...can I see you again?" Edward scanned her face intently.

"Um..."

"Please?" He moved forward and firmly took hold of her shoulders, his hold strong and resolute.

"Yes, you may," she croaked out and he smiled.

It's amazing but she has never done such a foolish thing in her life. Willingly as well she might add.

She had hooked up with a teacher.

****

"Had fun during your Spanish lesson?" Her mother greeted her the moment Alison stepped into the house, feeling tired and weary. She knew that her mother wasn't exactly concerned about whether she enjoyed the day. She was just asking her out of polite courtesy.

"Yea, it was," she fumbled, hoping her usually sharp-eyed mother wouldn't detect any lies hidden within her words.

"Was it fruitful?" She began laying out all the dinnerware and Alison could hear the sizzling of the vegetables in the pan in the kitchen.

"Well, we learnt all those greetings: Hola, despedida and tenur un buen dia, all those," she hurriedly said, reciting all those she could vaguely remember from the list. And then she remembered. "Mum, is Carrie back yet?" She silently held her breath.

"Carrie's in her room. She had remedial lessons apparently," her mother answered in a dull, monotone voice. Alison didn't know if that was a fake excuse or a genuine one but she was going to find out. She tiptoed to Carrie's room and knocked on the door.

"Come in." A muffled voice rang out.

Alison boldly opened the door, stepped in and locked it behind her. Carrie was sitting on the floor. She had changed out of the sequin dress she had donned earlier and was in her Mickey Mouse T-shirt and pants.

"Did you get caught for ditching school?" Alison tried not to sound resentful but it was difficult. Every time she remembered Jessica's taunting voice and smug face, she just wanted to rip that face in her mental image apart.

"No." She sounded guilty. "Apparently, they have been doing these for so long, the teachers kind of turn a blind eye to it."

Alison didn't answer. She was recalling what Edward had told her after the intimate kiss. The Mean Girls Gang was first set up when he was a junior a few years back and his then girlfriend, Amber, was the "head". Initially, it drew backlash from many people but some girls started craving to join it. Every time the "head" wanted to step down, she had to appoint a successor- usually the longest standing member. It was the unwritten rule that no student should incur their wrath if they were sensible enough and no teacher should openly punish them for their activities. It was even whispered that Jessica, the current "head", had used her father's money to bribe the principal to give them leeway.

It sickened Alison that her sister had taken part in this gang. "What did you do to get in?" she demanded.

"Er, no, I just proved my worth by drinking a can of beer," Carrie said hesitantly.

"That's all?" Alison raised her eyebrows. "They let you in just because of that?"

"Okay, Jane pulled some strings. She's such a cool girl." There was a half-admiring, half-envious look on her face. Alison personally didn't think Jane was good influence and she certainly wasn't little Miss Mary.

"Look, Carrie, I'm concerned about you." Alison lowered her voice. "You should get new friends and know more decent people."

"Shut up, Alison, mind your own business." Carrie's voice darkened. "I get to choose my own friends, not you. Just because you're older doesn't mean you can boss me around. "

"You misread my intention. I wasn't trying t-"

Carrie looked hassled. "Good grief, Alison. In Japan, I was forced to be Miss Prissy but I obeyed. But since we're in America now, I see no point in following any of those rules now." She glared menacingly.

"What the hell, do you know what you are sayin-"

"Obviously, I know." Her sister snapped sharply. "I get to do whatever I like here. Even if I get a tattoo or piercing, no one cares." She gave a blasé shrug.

"You're getting one?" Alison's eyes widened.

"Jane has her boyfriend's name on her arm." Carrie announced it, as if she was proud of her friend's doings. "She said I could get it done cheaply at a tattoo parlour."

"Stop it, Carrie!" Alison was horrified. "Do you know these... establishments might not be credible? Don't do anything you will regret later." She shook her head mournfully.

"Jane is right. You're always a worrywart and spoiling the fun for others." Carrie looked disgusted as she scrunched up her face in mock terror.

"Carrie…" Tears stung Alison's eyes but she ignored the stinging sensation. Her sister's betrayal and defect to the dark side seemed more real than anything now. "I'll tell Mum and Dad about it." She made her way towards the door.

"If you dare to do it, I won't acknowledge you as my sister anymore." Carrie smiled and eyed her with a meaningful look. "And I will tell them about Edward Kingston and you."

"You!" Alison shot her a baleful look and narrowed her eyes. "You're incorrigible and despicable." How did she know about…them?

"I saw you with him in the classroom this afternoon when I returned to my locker to collect my sweater." Her sister answered her unspoken question.

"WHY DID YOU DO THIS?" Her voice was shrill like a banshee.

"You forced me to. I think Mum would be more shocked when she finds out that you're involved with your teacher." Carrie's lips stretched back into a triumphant grin.

"Carrie Goodall!"

"Shut the door behind you."

Alison knew she had her. Carrie won this round. Then again, it was no longer a friendly competition between two sisters like in the past. It had become something potentially more dangerous for one of them and more risky for the other. Why did Carrie change after moving to Washington? Unlike her, Carrie was very happy to embrace her American side- perhaps more than willing but in the wrong way.

"I hate you," Alison spat. At least, she had the last word.

"I hate you too."

The last image that Alison saw was of Carrie peering at her newly manicured nails with a satisfied expression on her face.

***

The Dance

Okay, I know technically Caucasians can be geishas because Liza Dalby was one (I think) but they're less accepted so you get my point here.

1 month later...

Alison crossed out the last date of the month. August was over. She had been in America for one month officially. Still, she didn't feel relieved or happy because of certain....things.

"Alison, are you dressed yet?" Her mother hollered.

"Coming!"

She opened her wardrobe and gazed at the neatly hung clothes. Today was Cornwall Institution's annual school dance and everyone was excused from classes. Each person had to go with someone from the opposite sex and for the past few weeks, folded notes were placed in lockers, furtive glances exchanged between people and love cards started popping out of nowhere as everyone hurried to secure a partner. Alison was a little bowled over by the invitations. So far, she had received six requests from six different guys. In the end, she ended up going with Alex because he was her good friend after all.

As for Edward... Things were going fine between them. They had met up occasionally for dates and subconsciously, she was waiting for Edward to go to Stanford and quit being a teacher before they progressed further to prevent any tongues from wagging. Although she wanted to go with Edward for the dance, teachers were prohibited to attend with students. Obviously that didn't stop some thick-skinned girls like Jessica from sending flirty messages and placing love poems on his desk. Alison wasn't perturbed of course. She knew Edward wouldn't betray her but jealousy was a very dangerous thing and she was careful to keep away from it.

As for Carrie, Alison couldn't find any word to describe her. Ever since that fateful incident, she had been going home late and leaving the house early on the pretext that she was studying with some mates but Alison knew it wasn't true. Often, when she got a bathroom pass during the lesson, she would find her sister giggling and gossiping in the girls' restroom, as if oblivious to anyone else. She couldn't tell her Mum about Carrie because her sister would never forgive her if she did that. And there was that tiny matter of her knowing about Edward and her.....

"Alison! Be sure you're done in fifteen minutes! Alex is coming over soon!"

"Yes, Mother!"

Alison surveyed all her clothes dismally. She had bought a lovely emerald green dress but somehow, she didn't feel that it was appropriate for the occasion. Her eyes turned to the silk folds of a kimono in the drawer. As if it was a magnet, she felt hypnotized by it, took it out, and inhaled the sweet cinnamon scent. Could she wear a kimono to the dance? Would anyone actually laugh at her?

Alison hesitated for only a second before screaming, "Mother! Can you come in for a moment?"

***"

Now, you look like a beauty," her mother said admiringly as she hung back and observed her daughter.

"You think it's okay?" Alison looked at her reflection in the mirror. She was wearing one of the expensive silk kimonos her mother's friend had given her. It was nothing like some of the threadbare second-hand kimonos she used to wear made of crude rough material. This kimono was in a water-blue with swirling lines in silver to mimic the current in a stream. Glistening golden fish tumbled in the current with soft red petals of a sakura flower floating in the river. Her obi was embroidered in pale pastel green and blue. Alison's hair was tied neatly into a bun with a flower as a pin inserted at the side and her lips were painted red. Although her Caucasian face wasn't supposed to match the dress, her skin had always been clear with no freckles and thus from afar, she looked Japanese.

"Beautiful," Alison murmured as she twisted and turned, looking at herself again and again. Thanks to her mother who used to know a dresser and thus, had the basic knowledge on how to dress someone with a kimono, she would look extraordinary in the eyes of the Japanese.

But would it look good in the eyes of her American friends?

"I'm sure Alex would be dazzled," her mother grinned and Alison felt a little taken aback by surprise. Her mother had never expressed her emotions so...openly. Both her parents were very reserved people. Sometimes, she wondered if they even planned to have them, to have children or it was just accidental.

Noticing her puzzled expression, her mother's face reverted back to the original impassive form. "What's wrong? Did I say something wrong?" She frowned.

"I..I'm not used to you being so excited about me." Alison winced, afraid that she had touched her mother's raw nerve. She braced herself for the ultimate scolding.

"Alison." Her mother breathed. "We need to talk." Alison had never seen her mother that nervous before but suddenly, she was even more aware of how her mother had aged over the years.

From an independent American teenager who had grown up in an Australian farm, Helen Wright had travelled around Europe for a few years after graduating from Melbourne University. It was then when she met Alison's father, Richard Goodall, who was working as a small-time army official in a small Turkish town. In a spur of a moment, they had a small wedding ceremony and moved to Arkansas in America. After Alison was born, her parents upped and moved to Japan after her mother had accepted a job as a translator and her father taught English and Turkish to Japanese businessman interested in learning a foreign language.

Alison loved her parents but when she was little, she used to stay with her maternal grandparents who resided permanently in Texas (her father was adopted and his foster parents died when he was 21). She often found photographs of her mother when she was young- a pig-tailed girl with a heart shaped face and small lips. For Alison, it was hard to see the transition from childhood to adulthood for her mother and she wondered if it would be the same for her.

"Look, I know that I've been harsh on you ever since you were young but because you're our eldest child and we trust you," her mother said seriously as she gazed down at her dove-gray knitted sweater and black trousers. "And I know how the move to Washington has upset you but we know that you're mature enough to understand that we can never live in Japanese permanently nor emigrate there because we're Americans. We can never fit into the Japanese society completely."

"But…my friend, Etsuko, said that her father was American and he got a Japanese citizenship," Alison whispered. She remembered the sweet face of Etsuko, her best friend at Akura Junior High School and the afternoons she had spent at Machiko's house, just doodling and talking about their ambitions. Machiko wanted to be a Kyoto geisha because her maternal grandmother was one but she had to wait until she was fifteen to be legally qualified and train to be on after leaving junior high school.

"Why do you want to be a…prostitute?" Alison remembered herself asking Machiko.

"A prostitute?" Etsuko had taken a step back. "Geishas are not prostitutes! Are you saying my grandmother was one?" There was a horrified expression on her face which led to Alison hurriedly trying to explain herself.

"Don't they entertain men?" Alison, who was then only fourteen, felt a little confused. Her mother had warned her to steer clear of the Japanese teahouses and not talk to any of those beautiful geisha who wore dangling bright obis. When she asked why, her mother had told her that they were prostitutes.

"Yes, they do," Etsuko had said a little impatiently. "But their main focus is on practicing their art forms. They don't offer themselves to just anyone. My grandmother retired and met my grandfather who was a painter. A geisha is a respectable profession and they're an integral part of our Japanese culture. "

"Really?" Alison was deep in thought then. She wanted to be wherever her best friend was and then decided that if Etsuko was to be a geisha, she would be one too. "Can I be a geisha?" she had asked hopefully, hoping to get a giggle or a squeal of excitement from her friend because they always did everything together.

"No, you can't," Etsuko shook her head sadly. "My grandmother says that foreigners or Caucasians cannot be geishas. You have to be at least Japanese to be recognized as one."

"But I've lived here for twelve years! I know about Japan as much as you do!" Alison cried out.

"I'm sorry, Alison-san. It's the fact that although you behave like Japanese, you aren't one and you never will be." Machiko lowered her head embarrassingly. "My grandmother always says that it is no use to wish for something one can't have. Just remember that."

Remembering that scene stung a little. It reminded Alison of how she would always be different from Machiko however Japanese she was.

"If I remember correctly, Machiko-san's father married a Japanese woman. That's why they allowed him to have a citizenship."

"But Mother-"

"Just concentrate on your schoolwork. You belong here." Her mother continued, oblivious to her daughter's distress. Look at your sister, she fitted into school perfectly."

Yes, how perfectly so much that she actually took up smoking. Alison wasn't sure but she found packets of Marbolos and a lighter in Carrie's bag. Her mother must be deluded to think that Carrie was still the quiet and obedient girl. But then again, she knew that since her parents weren't particularly close to either of them, it was difficult to understand the problems they were experiencing.

"Carrie i-" She began.

"And I know Richard is very hard on you but believe me, he loves both of you girls a lot. It's just that his foster parents had always been very aloof to him and he finds it hard to express his feelings openly to his children." Her mother smiled fondly. "And you know him, he has such an ego issue. Even if he was proud of you, he wouldn't tell you that."

No kidding. It's hard for Alison to admit but although her father wasn't exactly sugary and sweet, nor did he showed affections to them outwardly, she knew that he worked hard so as to support this family and had never betrayed any of them. Putting aside the abnormal explosive behavior sometimes, he actually made a pretty decent parent.

"Okay, okay, I get your point," Alison replied uncertainly and smoothed the creases on her kimono. "Do I look decent enough to leave the house?" She allowed herself to smile a little. At that moment, she felt a sense of camaraderieship with her mother.

"Go on." Her mother pushed her to the door. "I'm sure Alex would be dazzled by you," she murmured.

"Sure indeed," Alison echoed.

Pity Alex wasn't exactly the person she wanted to impress.

****

"Wow, you look...." Alex's eyes widened when he saw her and Alison giggled. "Traditional? Conservative? " she added teasingly. She figured that if people bothered to laugh at her, she would just laugh alongside with them rather than be all embarrassed.

"No, really pretty," he mumbled appreciatively and snuck another admiring gaze at her. "I'm so glad I have the company of Miss Alison Goodall for this dance."

"You don't look half-bad yourself." Alex was wearing a black tuxedo (like all the other guys) with a red rose in his pocket. His face had no make-up on it (Mrs Kingston had probably tried to force some on him but he had refused) and the usual cheeky grin was in place. Surprisingly, he had exchanged his spectacles for contacts and he actually looked rather good. Noticing her gaze, Alex took the flower out from his pocket and offered it to her.

"For you," he said seriously while trying to not break into laughter.

"Thanks." Alison was delighted. "It's so pretty." She peered at the rose and touched the red petals.

Am I a gentleman now?" Alex had been trying to get both Angela and her to acknowledge him as a true "man" but so far, both of them were adamant not to add to his ego any further.

"Yea, maybe." Alison pretended to consider and then said, "Is the limousine coming soon?" She gazed at the endless cars speeding past her and she felt brilliantly excited in spite of her nervousness. Alex's father had come up with an excellent idea of renting a limousine to drive everyone to the school and so far, Alex and her, Angela, Jane (although Alison swore to not speak to her for the entire evening) and Carrie (whom she promised her parents and herself to keep an eye on) and their partners were in on the plan.

"Who's the chauffeur?"

"My brother," Alex mumbled.

"Edward's the driver?" she blurted out unknowingly. Suddenly, her heart quickened in pace and she desperately wanted to see her nobody-knows-but-she's-proud-of boyfriend.

"Yea, I told him that he could have hitched a ride with some other teacher but he insisted and said he wanted to see someone anyway."

Alex sounded confused. "Don't know what he meant by that. I think he's officially psycho."

"Me neither," she squeaked and secretly smiled. Trust Edward to say that to his brother. "They're coming now." He squinted into the near distance. Sure enough, the limousine was turning around the bend, inviting numerous stares from the passers-by and pedestrians. The soft engine purred as the car drew up in front of them and Alison noticed all the windows were tinted.

"Hop in!" Someone slid open the door and Angela stuck her head out. "Hello guys." She grinned and Alex raised his eyebrows before stretching out his hand and said, "Ladies first."

"Thanks." Alison smiled as she carefully climbed into the car without getting caught in her kimono. The moment Angela saw her, she gasped.

"Alison! You look beautiful! I never knew this was how you looked in a kimono."

"I was afraid this would be a little too unique for the dance."

"Obviously n-" Angela hurried to reassure her but someone sitting in the corner of the car snarled, "It looks like a freaking clown's costume."

Alison turned around. It was Jane Kingston, accompanied by a Mexican boy with surprisingly asymmetrical features. She was wearing a backless, strapless, short skirt which was no bigger than a skimpy bath towel. Carrie was sitting next to Jane with a boy whom Alison had never seen before. Carrie's date wasn't even handsome or good-looking. In fact, Alison couldn't really tell but the boy looked like he had a tongue ring. His hands were all over Carrie which was wearing an extremely low-cut silvery dress. When Alison saw Carrie ignoring her, she merely shrugged and went to sit on the extreme side of the limousine.

"Don't be impolite, Jane." Alex scolded his youngest sister before rushing off to join Alison and Angela.

Suddenly, Alison looked up. She had just noticed Edward who was sitting right up front in the driver's seat. He wore a tuxedo and looked as good as any day. He caught her eye and he grinned. Alison's heart palpitated even faster and she blushed.

How she wished she could go to the dance with him. Although she wanted to snog him senseless there and then, she didn't have the chance to do that and obviously she must remember that her date today was Alex- however platonic their relationship was- and that she simply must pay some attention to him. For now, she would just concentrate on having a good time. She turned towards Angela and started an enthusiastic debate on how the girls would look like flashing peacocks today.

****

"This is just....wow." Alison was stunned. The entire school's auditorium was drastically redecorated and silver pom-poms were hung up, shimmery and shiny under the spotlights. The area was modeled like a disco though it wasn't difficult to navigate across the dark floors with the help of the multi-colored lighted sticks. A long wooden table was set aside as the refreshment area and there were appetizing and scrumptious cakes and glasses filled with Coke and Mountain Dew. A large disco ball hung from the middle of the room, twirling around as pop music blared from the speakers.

"This year's so much cooler. Last year, all we had was a Halloween-themed party," Angela pointed out knowledgeably.

"As long as the food's good, no one's complaining," Alex grinned and as usual, went straight for the refreshments area to hog a few plates of desserts.

Angela watched Alex scoff down a pineapple tart before saying, "Seriously, Alison, why did you agree to be his date? If I'm not wrong, one of the school jocks, Albert what's-his-name asked you out."

"What's wrong with Alex? He's quite funny," Alison said defensively. She didn't like the way Angela phrased her words.

"No offence, but with Alex as a partner, I hardly think you would get a chance to dance." Angela laughed and stared at her, "So what are you planning to do now? Dance or what?"

"I think I'll just stand around here and wait till Alex's finished. Besides, I'm way uncoordinated with my hands and feet."

"If you don't mind then, I'll just go and have a quick dance." Angela smoothly sauntered towards the dance floor with her date, a boy who was in Alison's English class and Alison observed as they adapted swiftly to the song and was soon one of the graceful couples spiraling in the room.

Alison felt a little silly just standing there. Besides, her dress was attracting way too much attention as it is. She slinked off to the refreshments table and realized Alex had disappeared. Sighing, she sat on one of the benches, feeling a little awkward and out of place. She shouldn't have come. Abandoned by her date and best friend, she toyed with the idea of just going home now. Besides, no one else would ask her to dance anyway.

"Waiting for me?" A low voice by her ear made her jump. She looked up and frowned. A boy who was wearing a retro hat lowered over his face was talking to her. Alison couldn't even see his face because the hat was in the way and furthermore, all the guys were wearing tuxedo so there was no way to differentiate who was who.

"Who are you? Is it Alex? Are you playing a prank on me? " Alison stood up quickly and almost tripped because kimonos were very tricky to walk in. The boy's hands instantly stretched out to steady her and she inhaled his scent of aftershave. She knew who he was.

"Edward?" she asked happily and he lifted his hat, revealing his beautiful face. Alison felt like smacking him but she was just too happy to be in his arms.

"What's the hat for? Are you pretending to be Michael Jackson? " she teased.

"To cover my face. I'm not even supposed to be here," Edward murmured. "I was supposed to be standing guard outside with the other teachers but, for the one person I love, I just had to escape."

"They didn't notice you?" Her heart fluttered when she heard his words.

"I pretended I had a stomachache." His soft lips touched her forehead. "Besides, if I'm not wrong, Mr Vichy and the rest just started a game of poker and it was so very easy for me to slip away...."

Alison didn't even hear the rest of his words as she leant forward eagerly to kiss him. His hands held her securely at the back and she sighed with satisfaction. After a brief period of snogging, she placed her head against his chest and closed her eyes, feeling very uncomfortable.

"Where's Alex? I thought he was your date." Alison wasn't positive but...was Edward jealous? He seemed a little irritated when he mentioned his brother.

"The little glutton went off to polish more snacks, I guess," she mumbled good-naturedly.

"That boy." Edward shook his head. "I was getting a little jealous when I saw you two together."

"Jealous?" Alison lifted her head and her brown eyes searched his face. "Why should you be? He's like my best friend and your brother, by the way.."

"I haven't forgotten about that. Though I'm afraid he doesn't think in the same way," Edward muttered in a low voice- so low that Alison wasn't sure that she had heard him correctly.

"I like it when you're jealous." Alison resisted smiling. She didn't want to tell him that she felt safe when Edward worried about other guys liking her. This meant that she mattered to him- so much so that he didn't like it when a possible love rival wanted to covet her. The again, where did he get the ludicrous idea of Alex being a possible love interest? To Alison, he was a good platonic friend and he'll always be just that. This status would never change. Perhaps Edward was just worrying obsessively as usual.

"I suppose you would. Now, shall we dance? " he whispered seductively as he tugged her arm towards the dance floor and lowered his hat.

As much as Alison didn't like dancing, she was willing to do it so long Edward was there to guide her. They waltzed gracefully around the dance floor. Although her kimono wasn't suitable for such an occasion, Edward's proficiency at dancing and strong grip prevented her from falling. The soft music flowed through their ears and both of them were silent, relishing in this private moment.

Alison caught sight of Angela staring at her and Edward with a puzzled look. She felt a little worried because Edward's build was large and he looked too tall to be mistaken as Alex. Angela gave her a friendly little wave and Alison lowered her eyes guiltily.

"I think Angela suspects you aren't Alex," she muttered hurriedly.

"Shut up, and just dance." He grinned. He didn't seem perturbed at all.

They moved in little rhythmic steps in synchronization and Alison felt so at ease there, she was starting to relax and enjoy herself. Surely nothing can get better than this.....

Suddenly, someone tugged her silk sleeve. Alison looked up and was horrified to see Alex standing there with a bemused expression on his face.

"Al..Alex?" she croaked and flicked a glance at Edward. Edward instinctively pulled the cap down his face and disappeared immediately into the throngs of people.

"Who's that?" Alex was still staring at the spot where Edward had disappeared from. His forehead creased into crinkles. "He looks sort of familiar..."

"Erm, no, he's in my Psychology class," Alison rambled. Hurry, change the topic! "Where were you anyway?"

"Sorry, I disappeared off to chat with Josh," Alex grinned. "By the way, do you know they have awesome mango cocktails? The strawberry one are only half as good."

"Well, I haven't tried..."

"You should." Alex looked around. "By the way, what are we supposed to do now?"

"Dance?" Alison mumbled feebly. "It's the school's annual dance, you know?" Sometimes, she thought Alex was really clueless.

"Yea, so we...dance." Alex looked uncomfortable as he placed his arm around Alison awkwardly. She flinched at the close proximity. As they took carefully danced at a snail's pace, Alison didn't dare to look at Alex. It felt strange to be in another boy's arms- almost as if it was an act of betrayal to Edward.

"Alison?" Alex mumbled as the DJ changed the song.

"What?" She looked up alertly. Her best friend suddenly sounded so serious.

"Are you dating anyone now?"

"That's a funny joke!" She gave a shrill, nervous laughter. "Obviously I'm not dating anyone..." She wanted to tell Alex about his brother but Edward and she had struck a pact to keep it secret and it was going to stay that way.

"Look, Alison, I have something to tell you." Alex released his hold on her and he stepped back while nervously tugging his tuxedo jacket.

"Huh?" She blinked under the glare of the bright laser lights. The atmosphere had suddenly turned too...intimate. It felt strange to talk to Alex like this.

"I don't know how to say this. You know me, I'm not used to..." he mumbled.

"Used to what?" Alison glared at him. "Alex Kingston, will you please make your intentions a little clearer?"

"I like you, Alison," he said quickly.

His words hit her like a gush of cold water on a hot summer day. She tried opening her mouth to speak but she was simply too....shocked. There was no other word to describe her reaction. Watching Alex look sheepish, she realized with a sinking heart that he was not lying \.

"Say what?" Alison gulped. "You're.....joking right? Please say it's just a joke." She was almost pleading by now. If his words were just for fun, it would have been regarded as going overboard but she would gladly take it so long as he didn't mean everything he had just said.

But no...

"I'm not joking, Alison." He flicked his gaze away from her. "I really do like you."

"As a friend? As a friend, right? " She felt slightly hysterical and tears started streaming down her face, messing up with the makeup she took hours to put on.

Looking slightly alarmed at her outburst, Alex took a step forward and muttered, "Are you okay?"

"What's going on?" An angry and reproachful voice jolted Alison from her senses. She looked up and found Edward there, only he had removed his hat and was wearing a teacher's pass now. He must have seen, witnessed and heard their exchange. Alison realized with a sinking heart. He knew what was going on between Alex and her.

"Look, brother, go away, okay? It's none of your business." Alex straightened himself and grabbed Alison's shoulders. "I'm just going to talk to Alison for a moment."

"You'll take your hands off her." Edward shoved Alex and he nearly knocked into a waiter who was juggling a tray of glasses. Alison felt startled. Was a fight going to break out?

"Why are you interfering?" Alex sounded annoyed. Meanwhile, Alison held her breath. Was Edward going to reveal their relationship? As much as she hated that to happen, she would definitely feel much happier if the cat was out of the bag. After all, she didn't like lying to people.

Edward narrowed his eyes. His tall imposing figure made Alex cower a little even though he was his brother. "It's my duty as a teacher-in-charge to prevent harassment to any students," his voice was menacing and dangerously soft. Even Alison felt her knees buckle. Edward's presence had attracted attention from a few people and they were whispering to each other and pointing at them. Suddenly, Angela pushed her way through the crowd and arrived next to Alison.

"What's going on?" Angela demanded as she squeezed Alison's hand comfortingly. "Alex, did you bully Alison?"

"Obviously not," Alex muttered distastefully. "I was having a very private conversation with Alison until my know-it-all-brother butted in."

"What private conversation?" Angela looked interested and Alison rolled her eyes in spite of the seriousness of the situation.

"Erm…" Alex looked reluctant. Finally, Edward snapped into his businesslike mode, "Okay, Miss Weber, can you be responsible for taking Alison to the restroom and I'll speak to Mr Kingston here." His gaze turned soft and lingered on Alison for half a second before he snapped his head up and pushed Alex to one corner of the room. Everyone was silent, almost in awe at the scene until a new song started up and everyone drifted back to their individual activities,

"Let's talk," Angela whispered.

"I was hoping you wouldn't say that," Alison groaned.

The Eventual Talk

After grabbing a stash of mango cocktails and a few cookies, Alison finally felt better and he sat on one of the benches in the restroom which seemed to be suited for this particular purpose of calming down the deranged and Alison finally understood why.

"So spit, what's going on?" Angela focused her attention on her.

"Nothing's going on," Alison replied all-too-innocently. This only made her best friend more suspicious.

"What did Alex tell you?" Angela eyed her carefully.

There was no point hiding the truth from Angela's sharp eyes. "He told me he liked me." Alison sighed.

"Oh my god! Oh my god!" Angela screamed and grabbed her hands tightly, only to invite strange stares from some sophomore girls. "That's so cool!"

"How is it cool?" Alison replied uneasily. Angela's smile faltered and she frowned. "Aren't you excited about the news?"

"No!"

"There must be another guy in this triangle. Is that right?"

Alison stared back at her quietly. Angela always had a knack of sensing this stuff and her answer was no surprise actually. She was just worried about the consequences of spilling the beans to her. "Look, I'll tell you a secret but don't tell anyone. Okay?"

"You can trust me." The sincerity in Angela's voice was impossible to doubt and Alison relaxed. She chose her words carefully. "This might be hard to stomach but…I'm actually going out with Edward."

She quickly checked Angela's face just to see what her reaction would be. She was the first person in on the secret and well, if she was going to burst out in laughter or frown disapprovingly, Alison might as well just give up on anyone supporting their relationship.

However, much to her surprise, Angela exclaimed, "Alison! I've been waiting far too long for this!" She gasped and looked positively delighted. "I'm so happy for you!" She hugged Alison tightly.

Alison was a little light-headed as she drew back from Angela's almost vice-like grip. "What do you mean? Have you been expecting something like this? " she asked curiously, wondering how on earth Angela could have possible known about Edward and her.

Angela laughed. "Have you ever seen how Edward looks at you in class?" she asked amusedly.

Taken aback by her reply, Alison shook her head shyly. She didn't notice such stuff. Unlike Angela, she wasn't exactly a perceptive person. For the past one month, her classes with Edward were exciting yet torturous at the same time. She tried to avoid staring at Edward openly but it took all her self-control just to do it. And it certainly didn't help that every so often, she would catch him giving him a radiant smile. She took delight in the fact that this was an expression which was reserved solely for her. On one of their dates, Edward actually told her that he sometimes asked her questions in class so that he could hear her smooth voice. Alison didn't know whether to feel proud or embarrassed when she heard that.

"I suppose it's quite noticeable." Alison winced. How many people had noticed Edward and hers...special interaction in class?

"Yea, and I've always wondered why he was smiling at a certain someone." Angela giggled and her face turned somber again. "So... what are you going to do about Alex?"

"I don't know. I didn't even expect that you know." Alison personally felt thrown off by all these attention. She never thought herself as attractive. In Japan, none of the guys were interested in her and she certainly held less than a considerable amount of appeal for them. She always attributed it to her unattractive features. Suddenly, she realized that she didn't fit into the conventional stereotype of a Japanese beauty. The reason why she couldn't attract any Japanese guys' attention was because she was a Caucasian. Now, in America, she was suddenly in hot demand. She wondered if that meant she was pretty in an American boy's eyes.

Angela looked perturbed. "You and Edward are perfect for each other. But you have a lot of explaining to do in Alex's case. Have you told anyone else yet?"

"No, not yet. It's not the correct timing," Alison answered quickly. Except for Carrie, who was using this fact to blackmail her. But obviously Alison didn't tell her friend that. "I'm practically swearing you to secrecy."

"You can count on me." Angela high-fived her but looked worried again. "Do you think Edward killed him? I mean, I know Edward was going to have a serious talk with Alex but if you had seen his face just now, he looked like he wanted to drag Alex off to the woods and chop his head off."

Alison really wanted to laugh but given the current context, the severity of the situation was less than amusing. "I don't think he'll kill his brother, right?" Alison replied doubtfully although she knew that with Edward's temper, he was indeed capable of doing that. There was always that tiniest possibility.

"You never know." Angela shot her a dark look.

Eager to change the topic of the conversation, Alison asked, "Where's your date? Won't he be angry that you're spending all the time with me?"

All of a sudden, Angela looked dismal. "He ditched me," she said flatly.

"Why?" Alison was shocked. Angela looked really gorgeous tonight with her hair tied up in a bun and that midnight blue dress was simply stunning. Which guy would dump her for another girl?

"He went off with this junior girl. He just made use of me," Angela muttered. "That darn Josh only wanted to show off to his friends that he had a date."

"That idiot." Alison growled. No one would get away for hurting her friend like that. "Don't worry, there are tons of boys lining up just to date you," she reassured her.

Angela gave a weak laugh and put on a brave face. "Oh well, I suppose so," she said it in a light manner. But even Alison could tell she didn't believe in that. It also didn't help that Angela had a reputation of being a nerd. From Alison's one month experience at Cornwall, she knew that American high school boys often hook up with flirty cheerleaders like Jessica and not with people like Angela. Sometimes, she wondered if this social hierarchy would even change in 50 years to come. It certainly wasn't all that different in Japan although it depended more on your family's position and status. An ugly but wealthy Japanese girl would get more suitors than a pretty but poor rival.

"Let's go enjoy ourselves and ignore the presence of boys for this evening." Alison patted her on the head. "We'll just have a girls' night out," she asserted.

"Yes, we can do that." Angela perked up. "No boys, just us girls." Both of them looked more than thrilled to be rid of boys for at least one day.

"Definitely."

***

The minute Alison walked out of the girls' rest room, she was enveloped in the arms of Edward.

"I was looking for you." His voice was saturated with relief. Angela quickly disappeared, given them some well-deserved privacy. Alison wanted to go after her and comfort her but Edward wouldn't let her go and frankly, she didn't want to leave his side either.

"Is Alex fine?" Alison sniffed, breathing in Edward's familiar scent. It felt so good for this secret to be out in the open.

"I spoke to that damn bastard already," Edward growled. "He won't be speaking to you like that anymore." He sounded so confident.

Alison frowned. "Edward, Alex's your brother. Can't you show him a little politeness at the very least?" Edward's attitude towards Alex was something she had been trying to correct to no avail.

"He was messing around with the woman I love. Sibling or no sibling, he definitely isn't getting away with that." Edward shrugged and ruffled her soft brown hair. "By the way, I love the strawberry shampoo which you use."

"Please." Alison tried to pout but it was hard to resist Edward for long. His random little comments about her always made her day. "Aren't you a little too over-protective?" she murmured as she nuzzled his neck. She didn't want to admit that she was secretly delighted with Edward's words. This would only fuel his desire to taunt his brother. Although her relationship with Alex had become a little too complicated, they were still good friends at least and Alex didn't deserve all the threatening from Edward simply because of her.

Edward's eyes were dark and warm. "I can be overbearing at times but that's because I care about you." It was impossible to doubt his words and Alison hid a smile.

At this moment, a few sophomore girls went past them and casted a strange glance in their direction. Alison instinctively hid behind Edward's back. "Shouldn't we go somewhere else more private? What if someone sees us? " she whispered hurriedly.

"Don't worry. I think the entire school knows about us by now." Strangely, there was a triumphant expression on his face. It was as if he was trying to be sad but his happiness still radiated off him.

"What?!" Alison staggered back and almost tripped over her kimono but Edward caught her. "Why do you seem so happy about it?" she asked suspiciously, poking him hard. He was supposed to be furious and not, well, so delighted after all. Would he get a black mark on his record? Would he lose his job? Or.. would he...

"Please, Alison, you're a worrywart." Edward put on a face with mock terror before shrugging. "It's good that everyone knows that you're mine." His face glowed with unexpected ecstasy. There was no doubting the fact that he was relishing the thought of Alison being officially his.

"What would the others be saying about me? Would they think that I'm...I'm a b..." Alison couldn't bring herself to say the word but thoughts of Jessica and her troupe of fancily dressed primates suddenly made her more scared than usual. When the word that she had become Edward's girlfriend had spread, she would surely be target of all their ridicule and jokes.

Edward huddled her close to his chest. "Don't worry, I'll protect you." He pronounced every single word carefully and Alison nodded although her fear only subsided marginally.

"As long as you don't leave me," she muttered.

"I never will."

And as they gazed into each other's eyes, they were oblivious to the loud banter of everyone else in the party. They were so cooped up in their own world that they only managed to acknowledge each other's existence.

In simple terms, they belonged to each other.

***

By the time everyone returned back to school the next day, they could only talk about the party and nothing else. Some were groggy, after secretly drinking bottles of booze while others look sleep-deprived and trudged around the school in a zombie-like trance. Yet, this year, it was different. There were buzzing news about how a student was involved with a teacher and all the students and staff members were gossiping about it.

Alison tried to ignore all those looks as she walked to her locker. "Hey, Geisha girl ! Think you're that hot enough to hook up with Kingston?" A jock bawled out, inviting appreciative snickers from his friends. "A hooker is a hooker," Jessica snarled as she puffed out her chest and Jane hollered, "Alison Kingston is just Edward Kingston's newest play toy."

Alison had to admit some of the comments hurt. Fortunately, Angela protected her and acted as a bodyguard. The bad thing was, she hadn't had a chance to talk to Alex. Edward told her that he had left for school on his own without them and she wondered if this was a sign that he was still angry.

Pushing open the wooden door, she grinned when she saw Edward writing something on the blackboard with his perfect, legible handwriting. It was nice to be in Edward's class first thing in the morning. She hurried to her seat and Angela slipped into the one behind her. There was still fifteen minutes to go. Her eyes flicked across the classroom but she was sorely disappointed when she couldn't find the person she was looking for.

Ding-a-ding. The bell rang as someone entered the room. It was Alex. Alison stiffened and her eyes followed him as he hesitated in front of the class, as if he was debating to sit next to Alison. Looking defeated, he walked over to the desk next to her and rather unhappily, he plumped himself down.

It was now or never. She had to seize this opportunity to talk to him. "Alex, are you still angry with me?" she said under her breath.

At first, he gave no reply. The only response to her words was the flaring of his nostrils and the narrowing of his eyes. Finally, he cocked his head and eyed Alison speculatively. "No, I'm not angry with you," he said.

"I don't believe you."

"That's your problem then," he said with a careless shrug.

"Why are you so cold towards me?" Alison grimaced. "Even..even though I rejected your...invitation, I'm still your friend. Right?"

Angela cut in. "Hey Alex, you douchebag, why're you so obstinate? Alison just apologized to you and besides, it's not even her fault anyway."

"Shut up, pig head," he muttered.

"He's too stubborn for his own good." Angela shook her head regretfully and returned to her book.

"Don't mind Angela. She means well."

Alex raised his eyes and frowned. "Why did you decide to choose my brother?" His question sounded as if it was a mysterious puzzle he had to solve.

"Who else would I have chosen then?"

"Me, for instance." He pointed at himself without much abash. "In what way am I not as eligible as my brother?" he asked cockily.

Alison snapped, "In many ways, more than you would think of."

"Explain."

"Firstly, he's more mature than you," Alison said it as if it was an obvious fact.

"If you call having a monstrous temper as being mature, then I guess you're right," he retorted back caustically.

"Secondly, he understands me and he respects all my decisions and feelings." As if on cue, Edward seemed to have heard her and he raised his head from his work before smiling at her. Alison grinned back.

Watching their exchange with much distaste, Alex stuck out his tongue childishly. "Well, he's so assertive. I'm very much surprised."

"Thirdly, and most importantly, he loves me for who I am," Alison finished.

"And I don't?" he challenged.

Angela interrupted again. "No offence, bro, but if you think you are perfect for Alison, you must be pretty deluded," she added spitefully.

"You bit-" Alex started and Edward shouted from the front of the class without any slight hesitation, "Alex Kingston, detention today for repeating vulgarities and rude words in class. Report to Miss Andrea at 2pm today."

"Serves you right," Angela said quietly and Alison scowled at Edward. He was ruining her chance to patch up with her good friend. Why can't he treat Alex a little better?

Alex sweared under his breath. "Forget it okay? I don't want to talk to you anymore," he said angrily to Alison and turned away.

"But-" Alison cried out.

"Alison, it's no use talking to him," Angela said.

"I know." Alison sighed and stared straight out of the window. It was a wonder she was still able to maintain a picture of calmness on the outside although she knew that her inner self was turmoil. She hadn't expected Alex to be so sensitive to her rejection. Was this how teenage boys react all the time? Her past experiences didn't give her much to refer to. Why can't boys have normal relationships with girls without any romantic feelings involved?

Half a second after that thought, she slammed her fist angrily on the table, causing everyone in the class to be startled.

"What the hell are you doing, Goodall?!" An unfriendly-looking boy who was filled with animosity growled.

Edward stared at her with a thoughtful look on his face and Alison bit her lips in response to his burning gaze. She just knew that things had gotten a lot more complicated than she had bargained for.

Secrets Revealed

Feeling distracted and angered by Alex's aloofness and renewed coolness, Alison stomped out of the classroom immediately when the bell rang and Angela hurried to catch up with her.

"Wait, Ali!" she shouted, her voice echoing across the hallway.

Alison wasn't tempted to answer her. As she went around the corner, she found herself bumping into her sister alongside with her evil sidekick, Jane Kingston.

"Carrie, what a surprise," she retorted. She didn't know what came over her but after Alex's incident; she lost the need to be polite to her sister anymore. There was no point being nice to someone who didn't reciprocate any of your feelings.

"Alison," Carrie answered coolly as well. There wasn't a flicker of recognition on her face. Her once youthful and innocent personality had changed into something more beautiful and deadly. And while Alison saw her sister every day at home and in school, both of them firmly resolved to stay away from each other and keep their side of the promise.

"The bitch is here," Jane snapped unpleasantly. Alison felt a little sickened when she saw her. After all, Jane bore a striking resemblance to Alex despite the differences in hair color and seeing her reminded Alison of her brother which was something she repeatedly tried to forget. Funnily enough, in a brief observation, she suddenly noticed that Edward looked very dissimilar to his two siblings. He had a different hair color, nose and face shape. Perhaps it was just a coincidence but there were just no visible physical traits which Edward shared with Alex and Jane. She wondered why.

Angela caught up with her at that instant and her intelligent brown eyes instantly took in the two girls. "What's going on?" she murmured.

"Nothing," Alison gritted through her teeth. "Now, will you please excuse us.." She tried bypassing them but Jane stuck out her arm and blocked her way. "Not so fast, geeek," Jane growled, her blonde hair brushing against Alison's skin and the latter flinched before taking a step back.

"What do you want?" Alison glared at both of them.

"My sistah has something to ask you," Jane replied monotonously.

"Alison? Isn't that Carrie, your own sister? What's going on? " Alison whispered furiously as her words overlapped with the noise buzzing in the background.

"Bear with me for a moment," Alison told her and turned to Carrie. "What do you want, stranger?" she adopted a sarcastic tone. Alison didn't like speaking in this manner to Carrie. It felt so wrong and so foreign to her. They acted as if they were long sworn enemies instead of two close siblings who grew up together and confided in each other their secrets. Alison almost felt like tearing up when she thought about the happy moments she once shared with Carrie. It felt so distant and faraway now. Don't show any signs of weakness. Her inner self reminded her.

Carrie winced for a second but when Jane darted a stern look at her, she straightened herself and stared at Alison in the eye. "I heard you are officially going out with Edward Kingston."

"I suppose you would know best," Alison muttered bitingly and she could feel Angela tense up by her side.

"Well, what about Alex then?"

"What about him then?" Another unwanted reminder of her best friend. When was this ever going to end?

"Are you going out with him?" Carrie jabbed a hostile finger at her.

"No," she snapped. What gave everyone this idea? Didn't they clear things up yesterday already? And wasn't this supposed to be old news already? Why are they still harping on it?

"Then why does he say otherwise? " Carrie's lips curved into an unhappy frown. "I asked him out today and he said he wasn't available for anyone except for you."

"What?" Alison stared at her sister. "Are...are you interested in Alex?" she asked weakly. No way, no way.

"I like him," Carrie growled. "And yet, he had to like you of all people. Is he blind or what? Anyone can tell that I'm more attractive than you."

Alison gazed at her sister silently. She knew what Carrie had said was true. Although she was plain and boring looking, Carrie always had a lot of admirers and her fresh face was always inviting to any hot blooded male. It had never occurred to her that Carrie would have any reason to be jealous of her. Yet, somehow, Alison had unknowingly become Carrie's target for jealousy because of Alex's apparent infatuation with her. She secretly resented Alex for making things so complicated but she knew it was essentially her own fault. If only she had made things clear right from the start.....

"Sides," Jane drawled. "As Alex's sistah, I totally think Carrie's perfect for him so you have no right to fight with my sistah here," she sidled up to Carrie and purred fondly, "---for Alex seeing as how she has the backing of his family and you don't."

"Sister, my foot," Angela murmured indignantly.

"Shut up, Geek." Irritation burnt in Jane's eyes as she shot Angela a condescending glance.

Alison narrowed her eyes. She had never thought of the possibility that Carrie would carry a torch for Alex and she would admit that as her big sister, she didn't really like this idea. It was one thing for Carrie to get involved with a boy. It was yet another serious matter for Carrie to hook up with her guy best friend.

"I can't exactly control who he likes and if I'm not clear enough, I'm currently going out with Edward only and no one else." Alison's eyes narrowed into thin slits. "And I suppose it's your own wishful thinking that Alex might possibly be interested in you. He deserves someone better than you." Alison knew that the impact of her words would have such a great impact on Carrie that it would almost seem like she had slapped her. But she couldn't control herself. It was the only way she could pay back Carrie for what she had done to her and revenge was something one couldn't give up easily.

"You idiot," Carrie hissed as her eyes which was laden with mascara widened. "I will make Alex mine. You'll regret what you just said to me."

Alison shrugged, giving her a nonchalant glance but she could feel herself swelling up in anger.

"Let's go, Jane," Carrie mumbled, tugging at Jane's arm.

"So long, suckers," Jane bared her teeth aggressively.

Both of the girls flipped themselves over and walked off towards the opposite direction. Alison observed Carrie mutely as her sister disappeared into the distance. There was a tattoo plastered on her arms and she wore a revealing blouse and miniskirt. It was an ugly sight to below with Carrie bringing Jane, the blonde with a dyed pink streak in her hair, in tow. It was even harder to believe that Carrie and her had officially fell out and she didn't even know why.

"Sorry, Ali, but what happened just now?" Angela frowned.

"Nothing," Alison muttered.

***

"I love you so much," Edward murmured as he kissed her forehead again.

"Me too." Alison smiled wistfully. It was one of their dates and they were at a small diner called "Wendy's". The restaurant wasn't very posh but served decent food and most importantly of all, every patron could sit in a private booth so that no one could disturb them. Thankfully, while it was a Friday evening, there were no customers except for them and another old couple. There was just no way for anyone for that matter to spot them.

At this moment, a waitress came over. She was wearing a tank top showing a distinct cleavage and tight jeans and she smiled seductively at Edward. She was wearing a brass badge with "Laura" printed on it.

"Hey, sweetie boy," she breathed. "I'm Laura and I'll be your server today." She winked at him.

Alison threw her an irritated look. She didn't like the way this Laura woman was eyeing her boyfriend and she could see her eyes itching towards Edward's jeans.

If Edward had noticed Laura's flirtatious smile, he didn't display it. His eyes were still on Alison and he grinned to her. "What do you want?" he asked.

"Erm..." Alison snuck a peek at the desolate-looking menu. "Lamp chops and coke..."

The waitress responded with nothing but a nod and wrote her order down on a notepad unenthusiastically. Turning back to Edward with more interest shown on her face, she smiled towards him. "Hey, eye candy, what about you?"

Alison felt uncomfortable and she turned away. The gnawing feeling of jealousy was hard to dispel and it was becoming increasingly harder not to hurl the tomato sauce bottle at the woman. She noticed Edward still kept his eyes on her and he slowly shook his head, not even bothering to talk to the woman directly.

With an irritated sigh, Laura muttered, "Suit yourself." She then walked away but Alison knew that she would come back and try again.

Alison stared at the table grumpily.

"What's wrong?" Edward asked, sounding concerned. He placed his hand on her shoulder and whispered, "Why're you so sad?"

"I don't like the way the woman looks at you," she admitted truthfully.

"What do you mean?" he asked. Sometimes, Alison thought that as astute and quick-witted as Edward was, he was strangely clueless at times.

"I don't like how the waitress was so interested in you." Alison folded her arms across her chest. At this moment, Edward unexpectedly laughed.

"You're pissed just because of that?" he enquired charmingly.

"Of course," Alison huffed. Which girlfriend would willingly see another woman flirt with the man she loves?

"She's not even pretty." Edward shrugged and casted a distasteful glance at the Laura girl. She was leaning against the counter to show off her slim and slender figure.

"What does that make me?" Alison tried to joke but she was pessimistic. She wouldn't deny that the waitress was exceptionally pretty even in her eyes but she could never truly hide her fear that someday, Edward would leave her for another even more beautiful partner.

"Alison Goodall," Edward paused. "You're the kindest and purest person I've ever met in my life. I was so attracted to you because of your eyes which are always so filled with so much emotion. It moved my heart." He gazed at Alison and tilted her chin so that she would face him.

"Don't be afraid to tell me your insecurities," he whispered. "And I promise you I'll never leave you." He leant forward and placed his lips against hers. Alison closed her eyes and enjoyed this glorious moment. Ever since they started dating secretly, she knew that every kiss with Edward was so different. This time, the feeling was more sentimental and passion stirred within her. This feeling felt strangely comforting.

"I believe you." She brushed her hand against his hair, enjoying the soft texture and silky feeling. She couldn't believe that Edward was real and belonged to her. She felt so undeserving of him.

"Ahem." A loud cough emanated from someone standing nearby.

They pulled away from each other reluctantly and Alison blushed. Edward glanced up and frowned when he saw the same waitress.

"What do you want?" he asked politely though he wasn't exactly successful in hiding his irritation. "Has the meal arrived?"

The waitress plastered on a fake smile. "It's still in midst of preparation. I was just wondering, do you live in this general area?" She gestured with her hand.

Edward caught Alison's eye for a moment and he slowly said, "Yes, I live just around the corner."

"Do you work around here?" she asked cheerily.

"I'm a part-time teacher at Cornwall Institution."

"You look too young to be one," the waitress spoke a little too brightly. Her eyes lingered on his chest and Alison could imagine her thoughts running wild. Alison didn't like to deny this but she couldn't blame all these females. It was hard to not be attracted to Edward after all.

"For your information, there's no age restriction," he replied dryly.

"Well, would you, erm," the waitress fumbled. "-meet up someday and have a cup of coffee?" She extracted out a crumpled piece of paper from her pocket and shoved it eagerly towards him.

Edward stared down at the paper disbelievingly and his mouth hung open. Alison felt like giggling but decided it was inappropriate.

"You do realise, Miss..." he read off the nametag. "-Laura, that I've a girlfriend who is sitting right here." He put an arm protectively around Alison.

Not taking note of the subtle hint, the waitress was undeterred and said brazenly, "Well, if you don't happen to stick around long enough with her. You can always call my number." She winked again.

Disgusted, Edward crushed the piece of paper in his hands and threw it at her. "You'd better not repeat those words again. I repeat, I've a girlfriend and if you're smart enough, you'd better not mess with me." He glared menacingly at her.

The Laura girl scowled at Alison and strutted off, not even picking up the small scraps of paper. Alison waited until she disappeared from view before laughing.

"You mean person! You scared off her!"

"No, I didn't." Edward turned to stare at Alison longingly. "She was getting annoying and she can't possibly measure up to you." He drew shapes on her arm with his hand and Alison felt her insides tingle as his finger touched her bare skin.

"I bet all the students and women in the world are afraid of you," she teased. All her doubts had disappeared and after observing this incident, she suddenly felt assured that Edward truly loved her.

"You know, let's just go now," Edward spoke softly. "I can't stand the sight of that infuriating woman once more."

"What about the food?" Alison pretended to protest.

"Whatever, I'll just pay for it." Edward rolled his eyes and slapped a fifty-dollar bill on the table. "Let's just grab a sushi roll from Uncle Wong."

"Sounds good to me." Alison was secretly delighted.

"Shall we go, o-fascinating Miss Goodall?" He held out his hand.

"Yes, we should, o-great Mr Kingston," she chuckled. Together, they sauntered out of the restaurant- oblivious to the appalled looks which had appeared on the waitress' face.

***

"So....I wanted to ask you something," Alison asked cautiously as she took a small bite of her sushi wrap. They were sitting on the grass in a park and looking at the scenic view of the night sky.

"Yes?" Edward turned all his attention to her as he put down his Coke. "I'm listening," he said a little cheekily.

"Well, you know, Alex once mentioned that-"

"What did that imbecile brother of mine say?" he growled with his mood changing drastically.

Alison frowned. "He once said that…" she hesitated. "-that you had a girlfriend called Amber."

"Oh, that." His face turned expressionless. Alison took that as a bad sign.

"And he said it was the only serious relationship you had," she continued carefully and winced once the words were out of the mouth. Alison knew that it was a delicate and sensitive subject and she was quite sure that an unspoken rule exists whereby one should not mention the exes of your partner. However, she couldn't contain her curiosity and somehow, she wanted to know what events had transpired between this Amber girl, the love rival she had never met, and Edward and whether… they once shared something special although that was a forbidden thought she didn't particularly like to entertain.

Edward grew still and silent and Alison held her breath. Her worst nightmare had come true. She never fathomed that she would lose Edward to a girl she had never met but it was happening right now before her eyes.

"Edward?" she said in a low voice.

"Have I ever told you that I was adopted?" Edward suddenly replied, his eyes strenuously fixed on the constellation of stars in the sky.

Wha-What? Alison was taken aback. Why was he always sprouting new facts about himself? Up till this point, she still had the feeling that there were a lot of things Edward kept from her. Still, this new piece of information was something she couldn't temporarily digest.

"What did you say?" she croaked out uncertainly.

"I'm an adopted child of the Kingstons," he said quietly.

"How come-"

"You're the first person whom I told this secret to."

"Edwar-"

"Just listen to me, Alison." His voice hardened. "My history is a little complicated. I wasn't born in a happy and safe family at first.

My father was a drunkard and drug addict while my mother was a conman who relied on cheating as a means to survive." His eyes were closed as he relived his past. There were lines of tension etched on his face and Alison could only gaze at him, feeling utterly transfixed by his words.

He continued, "She conceived my accidentally. My mother hadn't wanted any children. Up till when I was seven, I was in constant poverty and hunger. I was always so scared that my father would come home in a drunken stupor and hit me while he was still stuck in that damned delirious state."

"Didn't your mother protect you?" Alison eyes widened with horror. The thought of Edward being physically abused when he was young was unimaginable.

Edward slowly shook his head. "Protect me?" he scoffed. "My mother only cared about herself and no one else. After I started grasping the actual situation, I tried plotting to escape but those attempts were normally unsuccessful. Every time I was caught trying to run away, I was locked up in the attic and starved."

An uncomfortable feeling settled on Alison. If only Edward had told her this tale earlier....

"When I was eight, the home welfare officials came to my house and rescued me. My parents were both charged for child abuse and they were locked up ever since. I was placed in a foster home and I remembered that every year, only the lucky few were adopted by families. The rest was given a basic education and were sent out to work at the age of sixteen," Edward muttered bitterly. It was impossible to describe the sorrow and anguish he had experienced over the years.

"I lived with the constant fear of being sent away. Finally, one day, hope came." Edward looked gratified for the first time and he pronounced the following words with reverence. "The Kingston was looking at the children and Mum and Dad selected me out of the few hundred kids and they took me home. Ever since then, I'm constantly reminded of how fortunate I was to have Kingston as my surname." A smile lingered on the edges of his lips as Edward recalled his family fondly.

"Then why do Alex and yo-" Alison bit her lips. She didn't mean to ask this question but she had always wanted to know what the source of resentment between these two brothers was.

Looking weary, Edward explained, "To Jane, I was probably a big brother she could look up to but for Alex, he thought that I had snatched away his parents' love. He regarded me as the favorite of the family and he resented me for taking away the status that was supposed to be reserved specially for him. After all," he laughed darkly at this point. "- I am only a mere orphan in his eyes and he is the true biological child of Mum and Dad." He didn't sound sad at all. His voice was calm, strong and resolute, as if he simply accepted everyone life had given him.

"You're so brave," Alison murmured.

"I'm no angel," Edward said calmly. "I know you're probably thinking how did Amber come into play. The truth is, I started dating her when I was entering my teenage rebellious stage at fifteen. The impression of how I was bullied in elementary school because I was unpopular always stuck with me. I started craving for attention and I dated Amber simply because she was the most popular girl in the school."

"What happened then?"

Edward looked somber. "After one year of being together with her, I realize I wasn't happy at all. All that shit, all that fake pretense was too much for me. I broke up with her and selected my friends more closely this time. The rest is just history."

Alison stared at him speechlessly. "Alison, are you alright? You're not going into shock, are you?" he asked worriedly.

"No...I'm not. It's just..too much to take in." Alison shook her head.

"I understand," Edward whispered. "I'm so sorry I suddenly overloaded you with so much information. But I...I can't help but feel so happy after telling you all these things. You wouldn't believe it. It's as if a burden was lifted off my shoulders." He sighed contentedly.

"I don't blame you." Alison hugged him as her small petite figure pressed against his warm body. "I just didn't know you had to go through all these. Why didn't you tell me earlier?"

"I was torn apart between those two choices. I was afraid once you knew my past, you would leave me," he answered sullenly.

"And you parents? What happened to them afterwards?"

"They're still living. My real father is in a detention center while my real mother is currently running a convenience store in Forks. We meet from time to time," he said regretfully as if he wished otherwise.

"Oh Edward," Alison cried out. They embraced each other and kissed, utterly absorbed in the heat of the moment. The last of the barriers between them suddenly vanished and Alison felt that she finally understood Edward. No one can blame him for whatever he had gone through but she knew that from now on, she would be there for him.

Never will he be the lost child who belonged nowhere again.

*****

Invitation

For the next couple of weeks, Alison avoided Alex. It was almost too uncomfortable to speak and meet him and mostly, she hung out with Angela in school while Edward was forced to sit with the teachers during lunch breaks. In a month's time, he would return back to Stanford after his internship was over. Alison hadn't broached this topic to him yet on how they were going to…progress further but she was sure that they would still meet each other regularly even when he moves away. By this point in time, almost the entire school knew of them – Edward and her- as a couple. Even if Principal Audrey and the other staff members were in the know, they didn't show it. It seemed as if for them, private affairs and official matters never mix together. At least this was settled. However, Alison hadn't exactly told her parents yet. Her parents just thought that Edward was kindly giving her Spanish tuition every Wednesday afternoon when in fact, they were half-dating and half-teaching each other.

"How do you say, "Nice to meet you", in Japanese?" Edward had once asked her during one particular session.

"Konichiwa, yoroshiku onegaishimasu," Alison replied fluently, ignoring the fact that Edward's hand was crawling up her leg.

"How do you say, "I want to jump your bones" , in Japanese then?" Edward murmured seductively.

That was the last thing he said. The entire session ended with them engaging in a heavy make out session and that was an unexpected twist in the situation, as always.

Reminiscing that particular afternoon, Alison almost smiled as she sat down at the lunch table. Although she truly liked Edward for his character, his physical attraction was an added bonus.

"Earth to Alison!" Angela waved her unappealing watercress sandwich in her face. "Thinking of Edward again?" she smirked.

"No way!" Alison said defensively as she bit into her chocolate cookie. "I'm not that love-sick."

"You should see yourself," Angela chuckled and she mimicked in an overly dramatic voice, "Oh, when is my darling Edward coming? Is he in school today or not? Is he in the toilet or not? Is he at lunch or not?"

"I'm not that pathetic," Alison muttered.

"Oops, the Mean Girls' Gang is at it again," Angela whispered and Alison looked up.

The bunch of cronies led by Jessica and her right-hand man, Jane was trudging viciously into the cafeteria. Apparently, Carrie had risen in position to be Jessica's second-in-command and for now, she was walking alongside with Jane with an aloof expression. Carrie paused briefly when she passed by the table where Alison sat but she continued to walk on as everyone else cowered in fear. The different cliques had mixed reactions with the MGG's entrance. The geeks tried to avoid attractive unwanted attention while the rest like Angela and Alison merely played the role as mere observers. The jocks, mainly in the Bad Boys Gang, were leering at the girls.

"Oh no, Alex is there too," Angela said. Alison bore her eyes into Alex's back figure. After they fell out, Alex had taken to sitting with the BBG and she was getting worried that he would be negatively influenced as well.

"Is Alex still mad at me?" Alison asked. As much as she didn't like to admit it, she missed having happy-go-lucky Alex as her friend. Now, she just hung out with Angela only and it got lonely at times when Angela wasn't available. Furthermore, Alison didn't see how offending two of the Kingstons and being in love with one of them was going to help. Conflicts often arose between them and it was difficult for prevent it from breaking out into a fight. From her angle, Alison could see Carrie eyeing Alex speculatively while her ex-best friend seemed unperturbed by her. Perhaps Carrie would have to work harder to win Alex's affection, she noted.

Angela sighed. "He's not the type who would apologize first. Besides, he seems bent on joining the BGG. Maybe he got tired of hanging out with uncool, ordinary people like us." Angela sounded a tad too forlorn and hurt which didn't seem to be like her usual character at all.

Alison didn't say a single word. Her eyes followed Alex as he got up to dump his uneaten food into the waste bin. The moment he caught sight of Alison staring at him, he quickly turned away and pulled the hoodie over his head, as if he wanted to shrink away into nothing.

"Honestly, you would think that I'm some psycho maniac trying to get his attention," Alison said disgustedly. This avoiding thing was proving harder than she thought. Alex tried escaping from her as if she was a plaque but she wasn't willing to step out and apologize to him first. As far as she was concerned, she knew that she had done nothing wrong. She did what any respectable girl would do to an unintended suitor by rejecting him politely. The point was, Alex wasn't going to let it go. He seemed to have trouble accepting her being together with Edward and Alison wasn't exactly finding it easy to think of him as her "brother-in-law" although they were of the same age.

"You can say that again," Angela answered. "Maybe you should try to talk to him and get him to join us again."

"I thought you disliked him." Alison eyed her curiously. She had never voiced it out but she got the impression that Angela hung around only with Alex only because of her.

"Haven't you heard the saying that "The cat misses the mouse when the mouse is away"? I feel the same way, " Angela replied wistfully.

"I wish life wasn't that complicated."

"Yea, me too."

****

Slipping into her seat during Psychology class, Alison waited patiently until Alex showed up. She noticed there were dark eye rings and he looked pale. As Alex sat in front of her, she quickly took out a notepad and scribbled:

ALEX, what's going on? Are we still fighting?- Alison

There, the tone was not subservient but firm. Alison flicked it casually at him. He looked up with a distinct note of surprise and read it before starting to scribble. Alison was relieved. She thought that he was just going to chuck it into the bin and ignore her. At least this was a good start.

He flicked it back to her, almost throwing it at Robert.

DUH, we are. In case you are still unaware.- Alex The note read.

Alison wrote furiously and threw it back at him.

WHY??????- Alison

Alex chuckled- much to her chagrin- and penned down an answer whilst keeping a lookout for their militant Psychology teacher, Mr Harrow.

AS IF you wouldn't know. Why else would I avoid you all this while? Just because you're always hanging out with my brother.- Alex

I know what happened between Edward and you. You don't need to hide from me anymore- Alison.

At this point, Alex gaped distressingly at her.

YOU KNEW ABOUT IT?- Alex

Yes, I do. I just think your actions are silly and immature. Your brother has gone through so much and yet you're putting on a childish tantrum. – Alison.

CHILDISH? IMMATURE? Damn, I knew he would paint himself as such a pitiful soul. He's just trying to get sympathy from you. He's no angel. He's a devil. – Alex

Funny, Edward had once mentioned that he wasn't an "angel". She hadn't known what it meant.

What do you mean he's a devil? He's the sincerest person I've ever met. – Alison

You're fooled by him. If you had known what he did before, you would be scrambling to my side now.– Alex

Alison stared at Alex's written words with a shiver. What did he mean by that?

"Miss Goodall, may I know what's so interesting about this piece of paper? " Mr Harrow grouchy voice boomed as he stopped in front of her desk and stretched over to take the paper.

"Nothing, Mr Harrow! " Her quick fingers crushed it and stuffed it into her pockets. "Your lecture on the intricate workings of the human nature is just simply fascinating." She smiled innocently at him.

Mr Harrow surveyed her for a moment before saying grumpily, "Pay more attention during class next time."

"Yes sir," she said, feeling relieved.

Alex turned around and gave her a knowing, triumphant smile.

Suddenly, Alison understood what he had written. Alex knew something terrible about Edward that she didn't. But Edward had promised her that there were no more secrets between them. Could it be possible that.....

No, it couldn't be. She had to trust Edward. She would never forgive herself if she allowed Alex to purposely sow discord between them. Still, she got the hunch that Edward hadn't told her everything. The adoption thing still wasn't the full story. There was something crucial missing.....

And that something has got to do with Amber.

***

"I think you're officially obsessed," Angela said as they walked home together. Edward was away on a refresher course and Alex had taken over the wheel. Clearly, their current broken friendship didn't constitute free transport for her. So she took to talking to Angela to relieve the boredom on the way back to her house. Angela lived near just around the corner in a shop house above Starbucks.

"I'm not crazy, I think Alex might be saying the truth." She had shown Angela the contents of the note but her best friend just laughed it off as a joke.

"Please, Alex is just trying to seize and opportunity to make you as his girlfriend. That's how boys think."

"Still, I think it has something to do with his ex-girlfriend, Amber," Alison said seriously.

"Amber? You don't mean the high school dropout? " Angela asked oddly.

"She left Cornwall?" This was a new piece of information. Why hadn't Edward told her that? Maybe it just didn't crop up in their conversation.

"After she dated Edward, they suddenly broke up. She then disappeared from school for a week. When she came back, she announced that she was dropping out."

"How did you know about this?"

"I hadn't enrolled in Cornwall then. But this story has almost become a legend. Some speculated she had hooked up with some hot surfer guy on the beach while others thought she dabbled in drugs and ended up in rehab. These are just rumors but there might be some truth in them, seeing as how she's the ex-leader of the Mean Girls' Gang."

"Well, erm, do you know about Edward as a student?"

"Mr Kingston?" Angela wrinkled her nose as she tried to crack her memory. "He's mostly invisible, I think. Some called him the lackey dog of Amber. I'm so sorry, Alison. It's not that nice to hear your boyfriend being called like that," she whispered apologetically.

Alison knitted her forehead together. "Could something have happened between them? I mean, why did Amber disappear suddenly?" There was something mysterious about the part. From what she had gathered from numerous conversations, although Amber was the head of the MGG, she was an excellent student who was supposed to be the valedictorian of the graduating class. There was no way she would give up all these statuses and quit Cornwall suddenly.

"Nobody knows, even the regular gossipers. After those years, nobody talk much about it anymore." Angela shrugged. They had reached her apartment while Alison's one was further downtown.

"I've to go now, bye." She smiled. "And don't worry, I'm sure Alex is just suffering from teenage-crazed hormones."

"I wouldn't be so sure," Alison muttered as Angela disappeared up the staircase leading to her apartment.

***

Reaching home, she closed the door. The house was quiet. Her father must have been out working as an accountant at a small central firm. Her mother, on the other hand, must have gone off to the knitting club alongside with Mrs Kingston. The two mothers had strike an unusual friendship and they were often seen shopping together. Alison didn't object of course. It was probably much more favorable for her if her "future-in-law" would get along well with her parents. But then again, she wasn't sure how both sides would react or whether this relationship would sour the moment she spilled out the truth of Edward and her.

"You back?" Carrie asked stiffly as she emerged from the kitchen. She was eating grapes and apples as her lunch- her new regime. Apparently, Jane had insisted all the members to be a size two and even skinny

Carrie wasn't able to achieve that if she didn't stick to an anorexic diet so she got to consuming fruits only for all her meals. It would have been healthy and all but the fact that she was getting skinnier and skinnier until she was only a bag of bones was indeed worrying. The worse thing was, her parents didn't even care. Her father wasn't even aware that his youngest daughter was dieting while her mother was in favor of Carrie slimming down.

"Yes," Alison replied equally coldly. This was how all their conversations went for the past two months.

"Where's Mum?" Carrie enquired with a blank expression on her face. She looked almost like how she was in the past. Jane had taught her some ways to elude parents' suspicion or so as Alison had heard. Carrie always took out all those hair extensions and washed off the nail polish the moment she got home so as to avoid suspicion. And the tattoo she got was hidden beneath her long-sleeved sweaters which she wore to school every day before changing into something more revealing. Through this way, Carrie was able to continue her extreme behavior unsuspectingly and no one in the family knew except for Alison.

"Don't know," Alison said and started to head straight for her room.

"Just to tell you, Alex will be dating me sooner or later," her sister called out after her.

Alison stopped. "Does this concern me at all?" she asked.

"Obviously." There was a glint in Carrie's eyes. She picked out a card from her bag and threw it at Alison who caught it with perfect precision.

"What's this?" She read the glossy cover. "Why is Jessica inviting me to a party? Doesn't she usually invite only the MGG and BBG only?"

"You seem well-informed," Carrie answered smugly. "This time, Jessica is inviting the entire school including those pathetic geeks."

"Why?"

"Just to show how rich she is."

Alison muttered suspiciously, "And how does Alex come into this entire thing?"

"He's coming and if you want to patch things up with him, I suggest you make an undeserving appearance too," Carrie said casually, flicking her brown hair over her shoulder as an imitation of Jane's signature move.

"Is this some sort of trick?" Alison scowled at her sister. It was hard to not be distrustful of Carrie. She always wondered what tricks she had up her sleeves or whether Jane was imparting all her knowledge of deceiving people to her.

"It depends on how you look at it." Carrie vanished into her room, leaving Alison standing there all alone and looking foolish holding an expensive watermarked card.

***

As she stumbled back into her room, Alison heard the distinct tune of her phone ringing.

"Hello?" she asked as she flipped open the mobile cover.

"Alison?" The crackly voice of Edward could be heard.

"Yes?" Alison breathed as her heartbeat quickened.

"Did you receive the invitation from Miss Jessica Hampton to her party?"

"Yes." Alison felt surprised that he knew of it but then again, surely Jessica would love to show off to the man of his dreams.

"Are you going for the thing?" Edward asked.

Alison contemplated briefly. What Carrie said was true. If she could happen to catch Alex at the party, she could corner him and make an attempt- however futile it might be- to retrieve back a precious friendship. Still, she was a little worried about the sort of party Jessica was going to organize.

"Is it going to involve booze and drugs?"

"I'm not sure but I speculate she probably won't try anything dirty as the entire school would be there."

"Good."

"Does that mean you're going?"

"Erm...yes, I guess so, " Alison hurriedly said. "You're not mad at me, are you?"

"Oh no, you silly girl!" Edward laughed but his voice turned serious again. "I can understand the appeal how Jessica's invitation might be to people who haven't been to her parties before. It's considered a privilege, I might add. Still, I'll be there to protect you. You don't know how complex some of those characters would be."

"And you aren't worried about your own sister and brother?" Alison retorted.

"They know fully well how to take care of themselves. With Jane's bullish attitude, I wouldn't be surprised she would end up taking advantage of the guys there!" Alison could sense him smirking on the other side of the phone. "As for that brother of mine, I reckon he's well-trained in taekwondo to know how to protect himself from the bad guys."

"Oh, yea," Alison mumbled. She had forgotten that Alex took martial art classes every week.

"As for you," Edward's voice softened. "You are much too vulnerable and as your lawful boyfriend, I have to make myself useful, shouldn't I?"

"Yes, indeed."

"Well, see you at the party next Saturday then," he said.

"Bye." Alison hung up. She felt horribly guilty for doubting Edward's honesty. How could she think that he was keeping things from him? He's such a responsible and caring boyfriend. There was just no way was what Alex said true. Except... Alex wasn't the type of malign others.

Alison felt so frustrated that she flung her cell phone across the room.

"Why can't everyone just leave me alone?" she shouted and wept she buried herself beneath the blankets and pillows. Life would be so simply if she had stayed in Japan and not interfere with all these typical American high school melodramas. But now that she was tangled in this complicated relationship with Alex and Edward, how was she ever going to escape?

That was one answer she had to find out herself.

***

Party and Betrayal

"Are you sure you want to do this?" Edward asked in a low voice as he was driving his father's black Mercedes.

They were on the road and officially on the way to Jessica's posh party. Alison felt a little nervous and she frequently looked down at her clothes: light-blue blouse and jeans and wondered if it was too casual. Edward looked well-dressed as always even though he donned a similar attire as her-a new blue shirt with their names printed on it (which Alison had given him in light of their one month anniversary) and faded jeans.

"Sure, I am," Alison answered a little too cheerily. She didn't know what made her do this but she had this instinct (she didn't know if it was a female thing) that she was going to find all the answers to her questions tonight at this social event dubbed as the "most in-thing" which has ever happened in Seattle. They zoomed past the trees and Alison realized they were on the outskirts of the city. She took out the invitation card to check again and there it read:

Dear Students of Cornwall Institution,

You are cordially invited to the Party of the Year organized by Jessica Hampton which will take place on 28th October 2010. Dress code is semi-formal. Please be aware that dinner, music and snacks will be provided. And please be at least tastefully dressed unless you want the bouncers to kick you out.

Signed,

The Leader of the Mean Girls' Gang

The Queen Bee of Cornwall Institution

Top teenage socialite of Seattle

Future model and wife of Brad Pitt

The most beloved daughter of the oil magnate, Andrew Hampton and heiress, Rebecca Hampton

Jessica Hampton

Seeing the long list of Jessica's titles had initially made Alison snort but now, it caused her to feel even more inferior. She would never measure up to someone like Jessica and she understood why some people like Carrie and Jane wanted to be her underdogs. The prestige and honor of serving someone deemed as important was hard to resist. Furthermore, with the acquired power of being in the MGG, one could attain a certain social rank above others at Cornwall. It was just sad to think about her own sister succumbing to this forbidden temptation and desire.

As the car made its way down the driveway spruced up with fairy lights on the lamp posts to guide the visitors, Alison almost gasped when she caught sight of the lavishly decorated mansion standing inconspicuously in the backdrop of the forest. When Angela said that Jessica Hampton was hideously rich, she wasn't kidding. It seemed a little unfair that mean people like Jessica had everything others wanted but then again, this was life.

Edward swerved the car around and managed to find an empty parking lot. Even from outside the house, Alison could hear the constant buzz of conversation in the mansion and she gulped, half-afraid to face going inside and seeing all the people.

"Shall we?" Edward held out his crook of his arm.

"Yes, let's," Alison placed her arm around him.

****

What struck Alison the most when she stepped into the mansion was not how classy it looked but rather, how gothic the house was. There were no chandeliers, expensive vases and ornaments or collectors' paintings as she had expected. The walls were painted black and the floor was carpeted. A large black oak wood dining table stood in the living room alongside with black sofas placed strategically at prominent positions. All in all, it seemed like a painting extracted from the famous novel, Dracula.

"This is so..." Alison hesitated.

"Incredible?" Edward offered.

"Yes, definitely," she agreed.

There were streams of people around and Alison struck up a conversation with some of the geeks who were brave (or rather, curious enough) to come. She was in the midst of talking to a boy about Star Wars and Darth Vader when suddenly, Jessica strode into the room with her cronies.

Every one parted to give way to them. Jessica looked ridiculously satisfied as she saw the huge turnout. Jane looked bored; there was no better word to describe her. She seemed restless and her eyes kept flicking around- as if she was waiting for a fight to break out so that she can intervene. Carrie wasn't in sight. Her usual position was occupied by another girl with big buck teeth.

As Alison strained her neck to find her sister, she also noticed Alex wasn't there either. Was it just a mere coincidence? Or was she simply getting more paranoid than usual?

"Where's Miss Weber, urh, I mean, Angela?" Edward asked uncomfortably. He wasn't used to addressing his students by their first names even though he was only technically three years older than them.

"She couldn't come. She was down with flu," Alison lied convincingly. She didn't bother to say that Angela wasn't exactly happy about her turning up for this event either and she had even tried to dissuade her from going.

"I see." Edward looked around and he froze. "Miss Hampton is coming over," he hissed in a low voice, sounding a little like James Bond.

Alison whipped around and found Jessica heading towards her, or rather, Edward, with Jane.

"So happy to have you hear, Ed," she greeted alluringly and batted her long eyelashes.

"Good to see you, Miss Hampton," Edward replied, tightening her grip on Alison.

"Call me, Jessica or Jess, whichever way you want," Jessica purred. Instead, Jane rolled her eyes and acknowledged her brother with much lesser enthusiasm. "Hey brother," she said. Her attention flipped to Alison and she said rather grudgingly, "Hello."

Alison responded with only a nod and asked accommodatingly, "Has anyone of you seen Alex?"

She heard Edward growl under his breath but she ignored it. Jessica's grin widened conceitedly when she heard her words.

"Alex just hooked up with another girl. He was having quite a few cocktail martinis there..." Jessica trailed off purposely.

"Which girl? " Alison couldn't help but ask again in an awkward rush.

"Someone prettier than you, of course," Jessica fixed a smug smile on her.

Alison looked a little aggrieved as her eyes travel nervously to the closed bedrooms on the second floor and back. She didn't know if she had misinterpreted Jessica's words but she was quite sure that the only respectable place for heavy snogging was apparently in the private chambers. Yet... she couldn't very well barge into the room and demand for Alex to come out, couldn't she?

As if sensing her discomfort, Jessica raised her perfectly trimmed eyebrows and said triumphantly, "Of course, it wouldn't be good to interrupt them while they're in midst of some.... intense activity, as I'll tactfully put it. Won't you agree, Jane?"

"Yea, Jess, you're so totally right as usual," Jane giggled.

It is no use getting mad at them. Alison reminded herself feverishly.

"So, Edward, shall I get you a drink? Someone is practically dying to meet you." Jessica turns to Edward brightly.

"Who?" His interest was piqued.

"Someone whom you know very well." Jessica exchanged a meaningful look with Jane. Alison wasn't even bothered by all the talk. Her mind was just whirling around, trying to digest Jessica's taunts.

"You don't mind, Alison, if I go away and chat for a moment?" Edward asked, apparently concerned.

"Of course she doesn't mind, won't you, Alison?" Jessica butted in.

"It's fine." Alison said impatiently. With one last look, Edward reluctantly allowed Jessica to lead him away. Alison then pushed her way through the throngs of people and climbed up the stairs, occasionally tripping over the steps. She suddenly found herself on the second level of the mansion. Downstairs, she could hear shrieks of laughter and chatter but here, it was eerily quiet. Not that she didn't welcome it of course. The strange tranquility allowed her to assemble her frenzy thoughts for a second. She tried to not be intimidated by the expensive furnishing and held her breath as she listened for any noise or sound.

"Hehe, you're so good at this." She heard a girl murmur.

Hesitantly, Alison approached the first door and without any conscious thought, knocked on the door. There was a sudden shuffling of the feet and a man with a grouchy voice shouted, "Who's there?"

"Sorry, is... Alex there?" Alison called out uncertainly.

Suddenly, the door whipped open and a boy, whom Alison could only vaguely recognize, stared at her. With a sudden realization, she realized it was the head of the BBG, Robert. He was wearing a bathrobe and there was a very naked girl standing behind him.

"What is it?" Irritation flashed across his face.

"Erm..." Alison grimaced, half-wishing she hadn't been so reckless and interrupted in the middle of someone else's love-making session.

"Do you happen to know where Alex is?" she repeated, taking her chances. Who cares what Robert thought about her? For all she knew, he probably thought of her as a deranged and sick-minded girl who went around peeking at people having sex.

"How the fuck would I know?" Robert growled and slammed the door shut.

"That was polite," Alison murmured as she stared at the closed door, feeling slightly stupefied.

top being so stupid, Alison. Jessica was just bluffing. Besides, there was no way Alex would do something so idiotic as to have sex with an unknown girl. She comforted herself as she held on to the banister for support. She was about to go back downstairs when suddenly, a female voice emerged from another room.

"Hehe, Alex, you're so fun," the girl chimed.

Alison stopped short. No way, just, no way. It was impossible. This was just her imagination getting out of hand as always. This shouldn't be happening....

"I knew you would be mine. How does it feel to see my naked body?" the girl continued, oblivious of the fact that outside, she had an unintended audience.

Alison's eyes widened in surprise. She moved towards the room in question and slowly knocked on the door three times. No, no, this is just a dream. Her mind instinctively told her. She always used to avoid awkward situations and escape was the one channel she routinely used. But this time, Alison didn't feel like escaping. To put it bluntly, there was no way to delve out of this situation. If only she was wrong about her intuition...

"Who is it?" the girl answered in an annoyed voice.

"I'm one of the servants," Alison hastily made up an excuse. She didn't know if Jessica had maids or anything but she was taking a real bet on it.

"Coming," the girl called out and the door suddenly whipped open.

Alison glared at the girl in question when they came face-to-face. The girl's face was contorted and twisted in shock. "You!" she exclaimed in a frightened voice.

Alison pushed her aside and barged into the room without permission but she could care no less anymore. It didn't matter to her if she would see Alex naked but she was so overwhelmed by emotion that a sudden dizziness was enveloping her mind.

A boy was lying on the bed. Thankfully his naked body was covered by the huge fluffy blanket sheets. His eyes were glazed over and he was in a trance thanks to the subduing effect of alcohol. Upon seeing Alison, he groggily sat up and peered at her.

"Who are you?" he asked warily.

"Alex! It's me, Alison, your best friend!" Alison sobbed.

"Alison?" Hearing her name made Alex suddenly bolt up. Comprehension lighted up his face. Alex glanced down at his body and he looked horrified. "Why am I naked?" he gasped.

He's bluffing. He's acting as if he doesn't know a thing but in truth, he betrayed you. Her inner conscience was telling her that. She breathed in deeply and said in a steely voice, "Alex, we're done. I'm never ever going to talk to you again."

"What have I done?" Alex sounded confused. "Shit. I'm not even sure what I did to make you angry. And why the hell am I naked? Can you explain it to me?"

"Alex Kingston, I can't believe you." Alison shook her head. The girl was still standing behind her, silently observing their conversation. She had thankfully donned a nightdress to cover her body and at this point, she emerged from the curtains and Alex recoiled upon seeing her.

"What th-" Alex exclaimed.

The girl released a shrill laughter. "I told you Alex, you'll always end up with me," she said and darted a baleful glance at Alison.

"Goodbye, Alex," Alison whispered and spun around to dart out of the door.

Running down the stairs, she was oblivious to the commotion she was causing. Everyone was staring up at her from beneath and their eyes were fixated on her. But just at that moment, the self-conscious part of her dissipated into nothing. She felt awful for witnessing such an embarrassing scene just now. Even in her pre-teen stage, she was once warned by the counselor that teens tend to do drastic things but she had never fathomed that such a humiliating event will occur.

As she reached the first floor, a hand suddenly grabbed her. She whipped around and saw Edward's distressed face. "Where the hell have you been, Alison? I was trying to find you. Would you believe who I saw just no-" Suddenly, he caught sight of her face.

"What happened? What's wrong with you?" he asked alertly.

"Oh Edward," Alison drew in sharp rasps of breath as if she was drowning and struggling to breathe. Her limp body slipped into his arms. "My sister had sex with my best friend." After uttering that exact phrase, darkness swallowed her entire being.

She fainted instantly.

The Fight

In her dreams, she floated on and on. Those visual images which slipped into her mind were vivid and realistic- there was blood, images of her family and friends and of herself. She couldn't fully grasp the situation. The last thing she remembered was of Edward's face and nothing else. She tried moving her hands but apparently, something was preventing her from doing so. The sense of numbness was a little discomforting.

"Alison? Alison?" the angel called out.

"I'm here." She wanted to croak out but she couldn't speak for some reason.

"Can you hear me?" the angel asked.

"Yes, I can." She tried saying it but no words came from her mouth.

"Alison, open your eyes if you can," the angel urged.

Yes, I should. Alison thought. But she didn't want to return back to the reality and face all the load of problems overburdening her. She just wanted to sleep and forget everything. Yet, she couldn't resist but respond slightly as someone's hand touched her. She recognized the firm grasp as that belonging to Edward and with the unexpected resurgence of love for him bursting out from within her, she unwillingly opened her eyes.

The first thing Alison registered was the sheer clarity of the lamps and the white, blank ceiling. She could smell the revolting scent of medicine and sickness.

"Where am I?" she asked throatily. Her throat felt so parched and dry. It almost hurt to be talking.

"In the hospital." A figure sitting next to her answered. She turned her head awkwardly and saw Edward, the love of her life, gazing at her all concernedly.

"Edward?" she hesitated. "What am I doing here?" The only thing she recalled was that she had attended Jessica's party. Something must have happened then.....

"You fainted," he admitted. Alison tried sitting up and she felt woozy. Suddenly, a strong pair of hands steadied her.

"Careful, love," Edward said as he pressed a button and the bed automatically adjusted the height. Alison leant back against the bed frame and smiled gratefully at her boyfriend.

"What time is it?"

"3am in the morning."

"Why aren't you in bed now?" Alison asked faintly as her eyes struggled to concentrate their focus on him.

"I couldn't sleep. I was too worried," Edward admitted somewhat grudgingly. After a long tense pause, he added, "Your parents were in the waiting room. However, they've gone home already. They insisted on not disturbing you."

What? Instantly, she bolted straight right up and was in alert mode. Flummoxed, her expression changed into something resembling dissatisfaction and unhappiness. "Oh no, what did they say?" she moaned. She feared that her militant father would go on a rampage and blame her for being so irresponsible and careless and her mother would end up lecturing her on how unladylike it was to faint in public although she couldn't possible help it.

"Don't worry. I handled them pretty well," Edward replied smoothly.

"You?" Alison couldn't help but sound skeptical. The thought of Edward, a mere 19-year-old boy although he was in truth a basketball prodigy too, facing her self-obsessed parents was a little hard to imagine.

"Oh no!" she exclaimed as a sudden errant thought dawned on her. "Do they know about us?" She gestured weakly at Edward and herself.

Edward couldn't hide a little grin. "Yep, the cat's out of the bag now," he said happily.

"Why're you so pleased about it?" Alison snapped. This really complicated things.

"Don't you understand?" Edward rolled his eyes mockingly. "I can finally introduce myself to them as your official boyfriend. You don't know the pressure I face. There's a lot of competition between the boys for you."

"Oh really?" Alison couldn't entirely mask her skepticism again. As far as she could tell, guys weren't lining up droves waiting to date her. Was Edward just joking as usual?

"Sure," Edward replied seriously and hesitated. "You might also want to know that....Alex is also waiting to talk to you too." Alex? Alex? Alison questioned herself. With a pang, all her memories came flooding back to her.- the betrayal of Carrie and Alex and the shock of knowing that they did it.

"I don't want to see him," Alison said obstinately.

Edward eyed her speculatively before murmuring, "I heard about what happened. As his brother, I think you should also give him a chance to explain. And your sister too."

"Why're you speaking up for him?" Alison demanded. She was counting on Edward to be on her side just this once. Yet, he was behaving as if he was Alex's good big brother.

Edward paused. "I empathize him. I know how it feels like to be misunderstood by someone..." he trailed off.

"What?" Alison asked politely as Edward snapped out of his reverie. "I'm just saying what Alex did was probably unintentional even though it might not be a pardonable act," he explained fluidly.

"How is my parents taking to this? Do they know...know about...Carrie and Alex?" Alison asked uncertainly. She hated the thought of Carrie in trouble although they weren't not on the best of terms right now. She wondered if her father was going to purchase a gun to shoot Carrie the moment he realized she had unprotected sex with their neighbors' son. This wasn't something terribly clever but then again... this was her father, after all. Expect the unexpected, that was a phrase that could describe him. Her mother on the other hand was less predictable. Alison couldn't definitely gauge her reaction but she was certain that her mother, being so consumed in the traditional ways, wouldn't condone her sister's actions and would do something equally drastic.

"No, they don't," Edward answered immediately. "I must say, Miss Hampton covered up convincingly for your sister." He pronounced the name disagreeably as if it was a rotting stale fish.

"I still can't believe my own sister had sex," she spat out angrily. If only she wasn't confined to the hospital bed, she would have gotten up and expressed her anger physically.

"Me too," Edward echoed amusingly. "I still can't believe my brother had sex. And as so it happens, it's such a coincidence that he lost his virtue to your sister."

"Yea, sure." Alison frowned. "If this had happened in Japan, tongues would be wagging about our family. Is anyone actually going to treat this scandal as a gossip?" She wasn't sure how the typical Americans would react but for the first time, she felt relieved being in a more liberal society which was more accepting to such acts. She shuddered when she thought how her Japanese friends would have viewed her if they had heard of her sister doing such an atrocious thing…

"Please, Alison, we don't live in the Stone age." Edward laughed in his usual, deep, throaty voice that always made her body tingle. "Such things happen every time. They'll probably forget about in in a day to come."

"Wait." Alison frowned. She suddenly thought of something. To her, it was a sensitive topic and if she was in her mother's shoes, she would probably have died from embarrassment then blurt out the question to a boy but since she was in a "modern" period, she might as well just risk being a laughing stock and ask.

She looked at him in the eye and asked with a straight face, "Edward…erm… is your virtue still intact?"

There was a beat of silence. Edward's grin widened considerably and he threw back his head in laughter. Alison stared at him. How could he be laughing? This was a serious matter, well, to her at least. Or…maybe he was so amused because he had done it before…

"Edward, you didn't do it with Amber right?" Alison asked. She wasn't sure what she would do but to know that this beauty whom she had never known before had once taken away something from Edward that she would never ever possess herself was enough to make her entire being hysterical.

"Does it actually matter?"

"Yes, it does!" Alison cried out as the monitor started beeping furiously as her heartbeat went faster and faster. Her blood pressure was also increasing rapidly too.

"Alison!" Edward stared at the screen, looking horrified. "Do I need to call the doctor?" He started heading towards the door.

"If you do, I'll never talk to you again," Alison threatened as she tried to plug the drip out from her arm. Edward rushed to her side and pinned her down.

"Can you stop acting in such a childish manner?" The humor was gone from his face.

"Give me a definite answer."

"What do you want to know?"

"Did you or did you not lose your virtue to Amber?" Alison demanded persistently.

"So what if I did?" Edward challenged.

"Is that a confirmation?"

"Why are you so fucking obsessed with it? Who cares who you did it with?" He rolled his eyes.

"I care." Alison clutched her chest, breathing hard. "It saddens me if I realize my boyfriend had given his most precious thing to another girl."

"Please, Alison, you're in fucking America, right now," Edward growled. "This is not Japan and we're not as conservative as your darling Japanese friends."

"Does that mean all Americans have to have sex before they're an adult then?" Alison retorted as the tears clouded her vision. Why was Edward so insensitive? Hadn't he realized that to many people, one's virtue is the most important thing? How can he so callously and carelessly throw it away to some random girl? If this was just some liberal American thing, she would just hurl herself at him.

Edward looked furious. "Alison, can we drop this topic please?" he insisted.

"Give me an answer. Just one word." Alison wasn't going to back down. Maybe it was a female thing but suddenly, his answer seemed to matter a lot to her. Or maybe it was because of the fact that he looked so shifty and reluctant as if he was trying to avoid replying to her question.

A knock on the door startled both of them. Edward's face grew stiff as a nurse entered the room.

"More pain medication, darling?" an elderly nurse asked.

"Yes, I think she needs some." Edward shot her a look which Alison responded with a glare.

The nurse proceeded to the IV drip and started fiddling with it by inserting some sort of drug solution. Alison watched this procedure silently but her mind was whirling with thoughts. How had a conversation about Carrie and Alex changed into something concerning Edward?

"You're done for now," the nurse said kindly before slipping out of the room.

"Now, will you give me your answer?" Alison asked the moment the nurse was out of hearing and sight.

Edward gazed at Alison, looking as if he was about to give up and comply. Throwing up his hands in surrender, he said in a strained voice, "Fine, since you're so insistent, I did it before with Amber. Does that make you happy?"

"Was she the only.... one?" Alison gaped at him.

"Er...no, I think I did it with another girl when I was seventeen before," Edward conceded. "But I don't remember what her name was."

"You had sex with a girl whom you don't know?" Alison implored.

"Hmm, yes." He sounded unsure.

Alison leant back against the bed frame in shock. No way, Edward had sex with someone else before and it wasn't with only one person. For all she knew, he was probably this sex-crazed boy who had never told her before about his promiscuous sex life. This just wasn't acceptable. Call her old-fashioned or traditional but back in Japan, the unwritten rule was that if someone had engaged in a pre-marital sex before, he or she would have ruined the honor and reputation of his family and causing them to suffer condemn and ridicule. This might sound a little extreme but in a society whereby the elevation of a family's position was dependent on honor, the Japanese can't help but be less accepting of certain things.

"Alison? Are you okay? " Edward looked distracted. Well, Alison couldn't blame him. After all, he had just blurted out his sex life to his girlfriend. How embarrassing can it possibly become?

"Why didn't you tell me all this?" Alison had to resist whining.

"I didn't think it would matter."

"Why…why did you choose to…lose your virtue to Amber?" Alison stammered.

"I…" Edward was unconfident for once. He paused as he evaluated on the best way to proceed. "Certain things just occurred. It was complicated and I couldn't control it."

His words touched a familiar note in Alison's memory. Were these "certain things" what Alex had implied about Edward keeping secrets from her?

"Edward, what exactly happened between Amber and you?" she asked cautiously.

"Why are you asking all these?" he questioned.

"Honestly, Edward, do you think I'm a fool?" Alison glared at him. "Do you think I wouldn't realize that Amber's brief absence from high school in her senior year had something to do with you?"

"How did you find out?" Edward looked appalled and nervous at the same time.

"If you have the guts to do something, you shouldn't be afraid of others gossiping about it. Tell me," Alison spat aggressively. "- what happened four years ago?"

"ENOUGH!" Edward shouted and got up, knocking down the chair in a hurry. He shot her a vicious look and frowned. "I'll talk to you when you're finally clear-headed."

"No, Ed-" Alison cried out as he darted out of the room. Edward's strange behavior didn't give her the answers she had expected and she only felt more confused than ever. Yet, their conversation reaffirmed that whatever Angela had told her was accurate and it told her subconscious instinct that something was very wrong indeed about him.

***

Family is Family

This is more of a filler chapter.

Three days had passed. Edward hadn't called her. Even after Alison tried dialing his mobile phone and even called his house on the pretext of asking him such school-related questions, she realized that all these attempts were futile. If he had the desire to avoid her, she would never be able to talk directly to him.

Today was the day she was due to leave the hospital and as much as she was happy to finally be back at school, Alison felt slightly nervous. Within two and a half months, she had turned from an invisible transfer student to one of the most gossiped people. She had already received 25 emails from her friends (and random people) asking about what had happened. To be honest, she wasn't sure herself. All she knew was that both Edward and Alex knew the truth but she couldn't bear to face both of them.

"Ready to go?" Her mother walked daintily into the room as she held up her daughter's luggage.

"Yes, mother," Alison answered dutifully.

"Is Edward here?" Her mother casted an eager glance through the window and seemed rather disappointed when Alison said, "He's at school."

After the talk with her parents about Edward, Alison was pleasantly surprised by their reaction. Her father was strangely amicable and he generally approved of Edward because of his "perfect stellar record" and as he was "a fine gentleman with manners" as quoted from her father. She didn't disagree for once because Edward was indeed a very desirable dating candidate. Her mother was also delighted. After all, her mother had worried obsessively about her not having a boyfriend at all and she frequently heard her asking her father if having a spotless dating history was normal for someone of her age.

"How is Father handling all these?" she asked as they walked to the registration counter to sign out. Doctors and nurses walking past smiled at her and she grinned shyly back, simply glad to be healthy and not treated like a sick patient once more.

"Pretty well." Her mother sounded amused and laughed.. "He's making lots of plans like having dinner with Edward, having lunch with him again and, oh, I don't know, maybe he's also deciding to have supper with the entire Kingston family?"

"And.. Carrie?" Alison probed.

"She's fine. I must say, it's funny how she doesn't seem to be surprised by all these." Her mother signed the form and then led her to the lift. The expression on her wrinkled face suddenly turned perplexed. "However, I noticed she seems to be going home later and later than usual these days. Is school very busy during this time of the year?" The ding sound signaled the arrival of the lift and they piled into the small space alongside with a few other people.

"2nd floor, please," her mother said briskly and turned her attention back to her daughter.

Alison fidgeted. Just lie. Make up an excuse. "Yes, everyone is very stressed out right now," Alison answered untruthfully.

"As so it seems." Her mother looked really glad. "Your father was saying how at her age, Carrie could be easily led astray and he reminded me to keep an eye on her. I was just trying to persuade him to that it was impossible, I might say, for such an obedient child to turn bad. Wouldn't you agree with me on your sister?" she implored enquiringly.

"Yes, Mother, you're absolutely right," Alison said conversationally with a twinge of guilt.

Her father was dead right this time. He had the knack of spotting suspicious behavior although this wasn't a problem in the past because neither Carrie nor she had anything to hide. Now, the situation was different. She had a feeling it wouldn't be long before her army-trained father was successful in digging out all the secrets which they kept from him. While it wouldn't bode well for Alison, it could spell disaster for Carrie because her father had the perception that groups like the Mean Girls' Gang and the Bad Boys' Gang were cults aimed to brainwash innocent teenagers. Carrie wouldn't be able to hang out with Jessica and Jane anymore (though she would be really happy of course) but who knew what her sister would come up with next to rebel against her parents' decision?

Suddenly, Alison wished she could spill everything out to her mother and not feel troubled by all these seemingly significant problems anymore. But she just couldn't. The words wouldn't come out of her mouth even if she forced herself to say it. At this moment, school didn't seem like a very appealing option. She hadn't seen her sister thus far but she dreaded the thought of confronting Carrie about the sensitive incident. Alison wouldn't expect Carrie to feel any remorse or regret but if only she would apologize, they could go back to the happy old days to rekindle their friendship.

Dream on, Alison. That's never ever going to happen.

***

"ALISON! ARE YOU OKAY?" Angela screamed across the hallway the moment she saw Alison. Running up to her, she hugged her and surveyed Alison from top to toe professionally. "You look well." She grinned.

Alison smiled back. "Glad that I'm back here," she replied crisply. "How's everyone else?"

Angela sighed. She knew Alison wasn't enquiring about everyone's wellbeing. "Your return is one of the hottest topic of conversation today. What exactly happened anyway?" Angela looked doubtful. "Everyone's speculating on why you fainted. Some said that it was because of your sister, Carrie. The last thing I saw were some BGG members placing bets on it. " The moment she caught her bewildered expression, Angela hurriedly added, "Of course, if it isn't true, you can just clarify with them and tell them you were under a normal fainting spell."

"It's true," Alison said quietly as they walked to a secluded corner so that no one would overhear them.

"What? Come again?" Angela stared at her disbelievingly.

"What they said was the truth," she repeated. She was only telling Angela this because she was her best friend and confidante. Being very mature and trustable, Angela was also in some ways, one of the best people with whom she could discuss her personal problems with and she usually came up with rather effective solutions too.

"What do you mean?"

Alison's eyes darted back and forth and she pursed her lips in a dissatisfactory manner. "Alex had sex with Carrie," she admitted.

"What?" Angela staggered back. "Impossible!"

"I saw it myself. Not the actual process, obviously, but Carrie was in the same room as Alex who was naked."

"You saw Alex naked?" A horrified expression appeared on Angela's face. If only this situation wasn't serious enough, Alison would have burst into laughter and fits of giggles.

"Not exactly," she hissed. "But the real question is : What should I do? I just cannot accept my sister being involved sexually with... my best friend."

"Have you talked to your sister?" Angela asked instantly.

"I haven't gotten the opportunity."

"You should talk to her," Angela pressed. "You're sisters after all. You guys shouldn't be bearing a grudge for so long."

"I'm not sure she's the same person I once knew," Alison sighed. "She changed."

Angela gave her a sympathetic look. "Everyone changes. However, just because she did all these doesn't mean she loved you. I can tell she's doing all these just to attract attention."

Alison instantly perked up. "Really?"

"Think about it, Alison, were you able to fit in better in Japan then her?"

"Yes," Alison answered. "But that has to do with character, isn't it?" Of course, Carrie was a more free-spirited person who didn't like to be restricted by many customs and rules so obviously she would find it harder to adjust to the Japanese culture unlike her.

"Yes and no," Angela said. "She probably felt that once she entered Cornwall, she could finally outdo you. But when she realized that you had started having more friends than her, and,-" Angela gave her mischievous grin here. "---that Alex fancied you, she became jealous."

"You mean she's doing all these because she envies me?"

"Exactly," Angela replied and looked weary. "And I would know because I have two older sisters."

"They graduated from Cornwall?"

"No, they went to some Californian high school until we moved to Seattle. But that's not important." Angela changed the topic abruptly. "What I'm trying to say is, you might not see it, but the signs of sibling rivalry are there," she persisted.

Alison registered everything her best friend said rather unwillingly. "But..." she said slowly. "My parents like her more than me. If anyone is supposed to get jealous, that one person should be with me and not her."

That touched her raw nerve but Alison was glad she had said it out loud. It was the unspoken assumption in her family that Carrie was the more favored one. If she had told her parents outwardly, she would have gotten a slap from her father and a severe scolding from her mother who would insist that "she treats all her children equally" but Alison knew it wasn't true. Sometimes, she had the gut feeling that her parents were disappointed with her because she always remained as a nonentity with few friends while Carrie was always more outgoing and popular. In a sense, Carrie was a typical kid every American couple would love to have. This was one reason why Alison doubted she would fit in better in America than Japan.

"Although you might see it in one way, Carrie probably views it in another perspective. Perhaps she thinks that your parents don't give her enough freedom because they think that she isn't as mature as you," Angela offered.

"But it's true!" Alison replied indignantly. "Look at her; she's abusing all her privileges. What on earth could she be thinking? "

"Exactly," Angela said with a small smile. "Her rebellious attitude and her physical involvement with Alex is probably a payback to you. I'm guessing she found a channel to vent all her frustration through the Mean Girls' Gang and I think Jessica Hampton and Jane Kingston might be the friends who influenced her to take such drastic actions to exert revenge."

"I...I have never thought of this possibility." That was an understatement.

"Maybe this would be the key to resolving all the animosity and differences," Angela added brightly. "You should try talking to her, and Alex too and find out what really happened. I'm sure that your speculations would actually deviate much further from the truth that you would like to imagine."

"Wow." Alison gaped at Angela.

What Angela had said gave her a lot of new introspective. She always thought that Carrie did all these because it was just well, part of the teenage development phase and everyone had to experience it at some point in time. On the flipside, she had never imagined Carrie being jealous of her. Why should she? Carrie was more well-liked by everyone else and there was nothing Alison had which she coveted- until Alex came along. At this moment, Alison understood the sheer magnitude of how love and envy can be destructive. Carrie liked Alex but he didn't reciprocate her feelings and it made matters worse when it was revealed that the object of his affections was Alison, her own sister. This probably sparked fury within Carrie and an intense wish to wield more power and authority in Cornwall then Alison. Unfortunately, the only available means to do so was through joining and rising in position in the Mean Girls Gang.

"Are you okay?" Angela asked, as if wondering if the sudden overload of information was too much for her to absorb at one go.

"Yea, I'm fine, thanks for the advice though."

"No problem. Always glad to help," Angela said professionally; in a demeanor somewhat resembling a counselor.

Alison was a little curious. "How do you know all these by the way?" she asked interestedly. Angela seemed very experienced and knowledgeable about this particular field.

"Please." Angela rolled her eyes. "When you have two older sisters who often fight for others' affections, you kind of get used to the situation and end up being able to recognize all the indicators to sibling problems."

"You sound like you don't really like your sisters," Alison noted.

"Well? What can I say?" Angela shrugged. "After all, family is family. You can't choose them but you still have to live with it."

The Ultimate Truth

The moment Alison stepped into Psychology class, someone placed his hand on her shoulder. She jumped and spun around and was utterly astonished to find Alex standing there with a chagrined look on his face. He jammed his hands into his pockets and he looked so out-of-place that Alison would have laughed, if only she didn't want to run away and curl up into a ball somewhere.

"What do you want?" she gritted through her teeth.

"Alison, we need to talk," he answered, looking at her keenly.

"Now?" Alison glanced around the class. People were already at their seats and any moment now, Mr Greene would be walking in and barking at everyone to hand in their homework.

"Yes, now. It's healthy to ditch class every now and then." Alex held his hand out towards the door and Alison stared at it dubiously.

Should she? The rational part of her mind was telling her to stop, sit down, ignore this crazed ex-best friend of hers and pay attention to Mr Greene's incessant rambling. The emotional part of her was practically screaming: Follow him! Follow him! and already, it was winning over the logical counterpart.

"Okay, fine, let's go," Alison muttered and bolted out of the classroom. They walked over to a deserted part of the school's small garden. Nobody would be able to find them there.

"Well, so what do you want to talk about?" Alison said as she sat on a bench. Her mind was momentarily caught up with observing the falling leaves in autumn as they fluttered in the air around her.

"Alison," Alex winced. "I'm sorry for what I did." His gaunt face rippled with emotion and he looked as if he was about to cry- which might not be a strange thing except that Alison happened to know that Alex hadn't cried for at least three years straight now.

Don't be fooled by his tactics. Alison braced herself as she gnarled angrily, "Sorry? Why didn't you feel sorry before you did it with Carrie? You just sexually assaulted her without her freaking permission?!"

Alison felt a rush of adrenaline the moment she caught sight of Alex's stupefied face. There, he deserved this humiliation. Half-expecting Alex to bow down and grovel at her feet before seeking for her forgiveness, she was surprised when Alex shook her head and said, "You're wrong."

"Explain," she snapped. "Are you making excuses again?"

"I'll admit, both of us were delirious after consuming cans and cans of alcohol and we did it in a moment of folly but that does not mean that I took advantage of her," Alex said softly. "You're mistaken if you think I would ever voluntarily betray you by hurting you in such a way because I...I love you too much for that."

Alison's forehead wrinkled and she yelped, "Love? Who are you to talk about love? You're only sixteen for goodness sake. What you feel about me is just a mere crush. How can it develop beyond that?"

"What about you then?" Alex shot back as his eyes flashed angrily. "Do you have the right to say that my brother is the only soul mate in your life? What if it was just a mere crush and your feeling fades away with time?"

"Shut... up!" Alison shouted. "It's different!"

"Different? How then?" Alex said mockingly. "As much as you like to deny it, Alison, you're giving the same excuses. Why can't you give someone else like me a chance? You don't have to restrict yourself to one choice such as my brother."

"You don't understand my feelings for Edward," Alison said hostilely although she couldn't help it. "We're serious to each other and we're certainly not playing around."

"Seriously?" Alex laughed in a rather menacing way, sending a shiver down Alison's spine. "Tell me, Alison, has he told you about his little affair with Amber?"

"He explained it to me already. They had a relationship which ended a long time ago. Don't you dare go around and sow discord between us." She narrowed her eyes at him.

"Did he tell you why Amber ended up dropping out of high school?"

"Er…well, no."

"Well, perhaps he wouldn't be so happy if I told you the truth," he taunted.

"Tell me," Alison demanded.

"You sure you want to know?" Alex smiled. "Both of you might break up because of this."

"Funny how you should worry about that when it's my problem," she growled.

Alex's eyes flickered to his feet and for the first time, he looked nervous. "Do you know that Edward had sex with Amber?"

"Yes," Alison answered with restrained emotions. His words racked up fresh memories about the fight which she was trying hard to ignore but Edward's words kept ringing in her ears : It's none of your business. It's none of your business. Was she so insignificant to him that he didn't care if she was privy to his private affairs? Did she even hold any place in his heart or was all the space taken up by that bitch Amber?

"Did he ever told you that…Amber was pregnant?"

No, what, what?

"My brother was responsible for it. Amber had to have an abortion so she ended up missing school for a while," Alex continued.

Come again?

"Of course, Amber had hoped to keep the baby but my brother didn't want to. She ended up switching schools because she couldn't stand the thought of facing him."

Impossible. Shut up, stop talking. I don't want to hear this. I trust Edward. I…do. Do I? Alison questioned herself for the third time.

"My brother met Amber at Jessica's party. Did he tell you that?" Alex looked up.

"What?" That was all Alison could manage.

"Amber arrived unexpectedly and Edward was well, astonished. They talked for quite a bit, just catching up with the old times."

"And nothing else?" Alison hinted.

"Nothing else," Alex said a little grimly, as if he looked disappointed. He closed his eyes. "Of course, Jane set them up together purposely, hoping that something would happen but unluckily, Edward didn't give in to Amber's charms." He chuckled slightly. "Even when Amber kept flirting excessively, Edward just steered clear of her and kept saying, "I have a girlfriend already, thank-you very much". I never did realize that he was the loyal type." His voice thickened with a regretful tone laced in it.

They remained quiet for a moment, each consumed in their own thoughts. Alison wanted to act blasé about it but she couldn't. The thought of Edward having fathered a child with someone else at some point in time strangled her and even as the cool autumn wind whooshed by, she suddenly felt hot and feverish as if she was stuck on a beach in the middle of summer. She never knew that the hidden love enemy, Amber, was so close. She might have seen her in a fleeting glance or even brushed against her briefly during the party but she would never have been able to identify her and given her character and nature, it was probably nature that she never did meet her.

Alison wanted to go confront Edward and lash out at him. Of course, being the gentleman he was, he would never retaliate and would still silently bear all her torrents. It was probably this knowledge which prevented Alison from acting rashly.

"Alison, are you okay? I'm sorry if this was a shock for you," Alex murmured, putting his hands around her as a comforting gesture. She didn't even resist. It felt nice in a way, so long as Alex was being platonic and not trying to take advantage of her momentary moment of weakness.

"Alex," she said in the most sincere voice she could muster. "I'm sorry that I hurt you because I didn't want to be your girlfriend. You have to understand that I love Edward and that is not going to change because I don't think my feelings for him are as simple as a crush. Even if it is, I wouldn't be with you because I treat you just like my friend, my own brother." She sobbed after finishing her short speech. Alison was so relieved that she felt a little light-headed because she finally got to say all her confessions to Alex and hopefully, he would be able to understand her intentions. Even if he didn't which was a huge possibility, at least she could say she tried.

A regretful smile lingered on the edges of his lips. Alex lifted a finger and wiped away a teardrop on her cheek. "Oh man, Alison, you always make me feel guilty, as usual," he said softly.

"Why?"

"You're just so...innocent," Alex sighed. "You could have rejected me by telling me to get the hell out of here or just fuck off but instead, you gave me the politest rejection since the medieval times." He gave her an admiring look.

"Well...I wouldn't say that it's so extreme...." Alison commented humbly

"I'll tell you honestly, Alison. For all my prejudices against my brother, I'll admit he's an honest and decent guy although he did do some pretty shitty things when he was in high school," he conceded reluctantly after a moment of contemplation.

Alison listened attentively before adding in a small voice, "Does that mean we're friends once more?" She held out her hand in an attempt to reconcile and make peace.

Alex stared at her outstretched hand for a moment. "After a second, he slowly lifted his hand and shook hers firmly.

Alison sighed with relief. "Welcome back, Alex." It was impossible to hide her euphoria. She felt like screaming, shouting or cartwheeling but instead, she forced herself to simply smile at Alex.

"I'm glad I'm back. I missed being friends with you." He grinned back mischievously.

At last, all that trouble with Alex had ended. Even if there might be certain moments of awkwardness and discomfort in the future, Alison was just happy to be able to chat with Alex like the good old times and relish the fact that even if they couldn't be romantic partners, they could at least be amiable good friends.

***

"Congratulations, Alison! Alex finally made up with you!" Angela swooned with delight over the phone. Alison had called her the moment she reached home from school.

"You should be glad too," Alison grinned as she tried juggling a plate of lasagna and a bottle of Coke. "I'm sure you miss his little jokes too. Don't you try and deny it."

"Whatever." Angela sounded miffed. "Have you talked to Mr Kingston…I mean, Edward, by the way?" she suddenly asked.

"Say that again?" Alison stiffened. She hadn't told anyone about their fight because of it concerned a rather touchy subject. It didn't help that she felt especially apologetic to Edward after the talk with Alex. It made her realize that she had over-reacted and worst of all, she had unknowingly accused of him still harboring feelings for Amber which was really idiotic of her.

"He was in a really moody state during 4th period Spanish. He started scolding everyone and I wasn't let off either." Angela sounded upset.

"How has that got to do with me?"

"Do you remember the first time he terrorized the class?"

"Yes," Alison answered as she ate a mouthful of lasagna.

She would never forget that scene. Sometimes, she was still in awe how that terrifying, foul-mouthed boy could be the same sweet and romantic gentleman. But then again, after weeks of interacting with him, Alison realized that the intimidating exterior was Edward's cool façade and merely an attempt to disguise his true self from others. He only revealed his other side to people whom he was close to and Alison felt delighted that she was one of the lucky few.

"Ever since he dated you, his manner changed. He was more patient and caring to the students."

"I hadn't realized."

"Of course you didn't. You were so busy just staring at him in class. Frankly speaking, I noticed you salivated a few times during his classes."

"No, I didn't!"

"Yes, you did." Angela became slightly muffled, probably because she was trying to restrain herself from chuckling out loud. "So when his attitude changed suddenly today, I figure something was wrong between both of you."

"You're exceptionally observant, my friend," Alison said dryly.

"Thanks but don't try veering this conversation in another direction because I'm not falling for that," Alison said. "So spit, what's going on now?"

"It was about Amber." It hurt just to utter that name out.

"His badass ex-girlfriend? I thought you guys were past that stage a long time ago," Angela questioned.

"I found out that Edward got Amber pregnant once," she said desolately.

"No way!" Angela was shell-shocked too. "Oh gosh, Alison, are you going to be a step-mum at the age of sixteen?"

"You have an active imagination. She aborted the baby," Alison answered.

In spite of the initial relief at this revelation, Alison felt unexpectedly mortified and sad because an innocent life was lost. She was torn between her morale and her selfish desires. If Amber had given birth to the baby, there was no chance of Edward ever completely tearing away from her because there was a tangible link between them. Yet, the baby was gone now, and while Edward can continue to move on with his life, he might forever be haunted by the fact that he had killed a baby, a life whom he was supposed to be responsible for.

"Oh my, no wonder you guys had a fight."

"Edward doesn't know that I know about his past. We got into a fight because I was upset he had lost his virtue to Amber," Alison cringed. Admitting this out loud made Alison feel a little childish for kicking up such a big fuss about such a trivial issue which paled in comparison to the real deal. She realized that she was slowly becoming more American and less Japanese than she thought.

"Alison, why would you do that?" Even Angela was awestruck and Alison had thought her best friend was conservative.

"Have you lost your virtue yet then?" Alison asked, giggling.

"Yes." Angela's reply was short and simple but Alison was bowled over. She stared at the phone for some time until Angela's voice cackled across the telephone lines, beckoning her to answer.

"Alison, are you still there?"

"When?" she croaked out.

"Er... last year?"

"How come everyone has done it? Should I be doing it too?" Alison was mollified. "Should I just... I don't know, hook up with some guy on the street or something? Or should I book a hotel room with Edward and just do it tonight?"

At this moment, she heard the doors to the apartment open and close noisily. Her mother shouted, "I'm back home! I found some fresh produce from the market and Mrs Smith told me that...."

The incessant rambling was mixed with the hurried footsteps of her mother to the kitchen. Alison imagined her mother storing the vegetables in the fridge and brewing a cup of Oolong tea from the depleting stash of tea packets she had painstakingly brought over from Japan. All these thoughts were just to distract her mind from the conversation.

There was heavy breathing down the phone until Angela said carefully, "Alison. You shouldn't be doing it just because everyone has done it. For me, it was an accident with some guy from my old form class. We were just goofing around but even I didn't expect it to become so serious."

When Alison didn't reply, Angela continued with a twinge of sadness in her voice, "If I could go back in time, I wouldn't have done it. The experience wasn't terrific or anything because I didn't love the guy in question and I was mostly curious. But since you have a choice in your hands, I think you should keep this gift for someone whom you really love. Most of us have done it simply because we weren't mature enough to make the right choices but you can because you're different. You grew up in Japan and you're equipped with values that might be deemed as conservative to some of us but it doesn't matter because not being the same as others is not inherently bad."

Alison muttered, "You sound so profound."

"I'm pretty sure they're all in layman terms and easy enough for you to understand." Angela reverted back to her original cheery self. "Both of you have to try and understand each other because you guys grew up in absurdly different cultures so there will be those inevitable tensions and frictions."

"I know, I know. I just didn't know it would be this difficult," Alison whined.

"Relax, ten years down the road, you'll find yourself having matured and learnt from these experiences. That's what my sisters said, " Angela answered lightly.

"Very intelligent advice. Thanks for your help, Angela. I wouldn't know what to do with Alex and you," Alison said gratefully.

"Tsk, just remember, we'll always be here for you," Angela said warmly.

With a click, Alison hung up and put down the phone carefully. She gazed at her own reflection in the large mirror which was hung up in the hallway and almost couldn't recognize the person there. Three months ago, an unsure and quiet girl would be gazing back at her but now, she saw herself as someone who was more outspoken and confident thanks to the emotional support from her friends and...most of all, Edward. She felt a familiar tingly feeling in her toes and she stared at her cellphone for a minute.

Slowly, she dialed the number at the top of her contacts list. Placing the mobile at her ears, she felt the ringing tone humming away and within two rings, a gruff, irritated voice broke through.

"Hello?"

"Edward, it's me, Alison," she answered nervously, desperately hoping Edward wouldn't slam down the phone in a fit of anger.

"Oh, it's you." He sounded accusing and Alison almost shrank away timidly. "What do you want?" The most feared Terror who was abandoned as a kind was back. Edward Kingston was gone.

"Can we....meet up or something?" she asked hopefully.

"For what?" he scoffed. Alison imagined his face darkening as he started clenching his hands tightly together in distress.

"To talk."

"I thought we were having a cooling off period," Edward said in a strained voice

"Are you planning to break up with me then?" Alison broke down as she tried desperately to stop the tears from streaming down his cheeks. She used to scoff at those girls who went into depression after being dumped by their boyfriends in those weekend soap operas. Suddenly, she understood how lonely these people must have felt. It hurts to know that you were going to lose someone whom you loved dearly and it was your own entire fault.

Silence took over. Alison wasn't even sure if Edward was there. "I know what happened to Amber and I don't blame you for making that decision to abort your own child because you were trapped by unimagined circumstances. I just wished... that you had been honest with me, that you told me everything so that I could share the burden with you."

"Alison..." Edward sounded incredulous and his voice thickened with emotion. "You knew?"

"Alex told me," Alison answered, her entire body trembling by now. "And if you decide that you don't want me anymore...I..I wouldn't resent you or anything. I do understand that you've a past with Amber that I can never erase but I just want to tell you...that...I love you in spite everything which has happened."

Sobbing, she released her cellphone and let it clatter to the floor.

"Alison? Alison?" Edward's voice cackled from the mobile but she didn't care anymore. She slumped onto the floor and stared at the phone until she heard a shrill ring. She jumped, thinking that it was Edward calling her back and her mind was momentarily blank as she worked out how to talk to him. But it was the tune from the house phone. Rarely had anyone called their house. In spite of her curiosity, Alison just sat there, seemingly expressionless.

"Goodness, Alison, couldn't you pick up the phone?" Her mother emerged from the kitchen with her head dotted with sweat and she shot her daughter an irritated look before picking up the phone and going all polite and formal. "Hello, this is the Goodalls' residence. Who is this calling?"

Alison watched as her mother's forehead pucker in frustration and her fragile body shook slightly. What was happening? She wondered. Her mother scribbled something on a notepad and the person on the other side of the phone muttered something for which her mother responded, "Where is she held now?" before nodding and putting down the phone.

"What happened, Mother?" Alison asked anxiously. "Did something happen to Father?"

"No, Alison, it was the police," her mother answered rigidly.

"Who was arrested?" Alison cringed. Her father's pride and undisputed honesty meant that he wasn't the type to embezzle funds or cheat anyone of their hard-earned money unless he happened to beat someone up.....oh gosh, was that it?

"Hurry, change your clothes. We're going out," her mother paused. "Your sister has been arrested for drug possession."

***

Arrest and Sentence

Even as they sped past buildings after buildings, Alison still couldn't wrap her head around the news. She gazed at the dull and monotonous landscape and skyline that seemed to fade away gradually as the next scenery arrived.

Her mother was quiet for the most part and she handled the news rather well and it was only when calling her father to break the news did she seemed to be in distress.

"Is Father okay?" Alison asked quietly a she thumbed her way through a battered copy of The Finer Arts of Tea Brewing.

"He's fine. I don't think we should be worrying about him right now," her mother replied as she kept her eyes on the road.

"Do you think he will kill Carrie or something?" Alison barely managed to disguise her immense worry.

"Alison! Your father is not a violent murderer!" Her mother chided. "He's not accepting it well but that doesn't mean he's going to do something so extreme."

"Does he have a gun then?"

"Well...yes, he does but that's not important right now." Alison thought she saw a smile flicker on her mother's face.

Alison turned her attention back to the window. Her phone buzzed and she flipped open the cover. The screen read: Edward.

"Aren't you going to answer the call?"

"Maybe." She stared at the phone and muttered, "I'll show you. I'll show you while and it just kept vibrating consistently for five whole minutes until it stopped. Alison instantly relaxed and shoved the mobile into her pocket.

"Who was that?" Her mother raised her eyebrows. Alison could literally see the bubbles popping out of her head: My daughter's crazy. She just talked to her phone. I wonder where she got the crazy genes from. Definitely not me.

"Just someone insignificant," Alison sniffed.

Suddenly, the car stopped and Alison blinked. They were in front of a small property which would have looked like a normal family house if not for the huge sign with the letters, "Seattle's Police Station" emblazoned in red and blue. The front door was painted a vibrant red (the first thing which came to her mind was: danger) with tinted glass windows.

"Come on," her mother grabbed her handbag and opened the front door without waiting for an answer, pushing Alison in ahead of her. The air was colder than outside and at first glance; one would have thought that the room resembled an office. All the furniture was black, white or grey and there was an overhead television hanging in one corner which displayed news from the Seattle Daily although the sound was muted. Nobody seemed to be paying attention to the television box though. A couple sitting in the corner was crying. The man had his arms held around the woman.

"Why did he do that? Why did he kill her?" The woman sobbed, grieving for the loss of someone.

In another corner, a boy was staring into blank space. His face was ashen and his eyes were bloodshot. Beside him was a man who strangely reminded Alison of her father.

"What on earth have you done? I painstakingly raised you and you have given me so much trouble since Day one," the man shouted. The boy didn't seem to be listening, though. Alison wondered what had happened to him.

"Alison, over here," her mother waved her over and she saw that she stood near the front desk.

The cop sitting behind the desk looked up instantly. "Reporting of crime, m'am?" he asked in a rough voice. The guy was wearing a standard uniform, but he had a lot of facial hair and sideburns for a man. Strangely, his focused gaze and serious face compensated for the dreary look.

"My daughter, Carrie Goodall, was taken here," her mother said grimly as she pulled out some documents and identity cards from an envelope. She didn't mention the words "arrested " or "drugs", as if she was preserving some remnants of her pride in front of all these strangers and the officer seemed to understand her predicament.

"Ah," he nodded. He pulled out a folder from under his desk and frowned. "Teen arrested for drug possession?"

"Yes, and keep the tone down," her mother hissed.

"Come this way," he got up and headed towards a backroom through a long corridor. Both of them dutifully followed him, and Alison occasionally passed by criminals in cuffs and people being led into custody. Sometimes, there were happy moments there too. One woman was clutching the hands of another boy and she screamed, "You're innocent, Harry! They finally proved that you aren't guilty!" Alison smiled at that one.

As the officer unlocked a door and shuffled them in, Alison had to narrow her eyes under the glare of the brightly-lit lamps. There, sat in the middle of the room, was Carrie, her sister. The moment both her mother and Alison took a step towards her, Carrie's head flipped up, her eyes held a dull, open stare as if she was in a trance.

"Mum?" she whispered and her gaze flicked to the next person. "Alison?" It was the first time in a long time since she had said her name.

"Carrie, dear." Her mother took a step towards her, her smooth hands outstretched as if she wanted to embrace her daughter until a female officer restrained her.

"Please sit down," the female cop said politely. "Both of you," she added as an after-thought. She decided to nickname the guy as "Officer Dude" and the woman as "Officer Chick"

Alison numbly took a seat and her mother followed suit. Officer Dude sat between them as he surveyed Carrie's profile. Her sister now had an official police record to her name. It wasn't good news.

"Mrs Goodall, it is understood that your daughter, Carrie Goodall, was found in possession of a packet of cannabis and cocaine," Officer Dude said professionally.

"Impossible!" Her mother slammed her hand down on the table, an unusual act given her usual timid personality. "Carrie, darling, tell them it isn't true!" she screamed hysterically.

The officer chick came over hesitantly, looking as if she was about to put her mother in handcuffs too. Instead, officer dude raised his hands in an authoritative manner and coughed. "Evidence is now being processed as we speak and rest assure, the police will not incriminate the innocent. At the same time, the guilty will not be spared." He sounded like someone out of Law and Order.

Helen Goodall's agitation visibly subsided as she calmed down before facing the officer again, waiting for him to speak. Officer Dude looked impressed for some unfathomable reason and he continued, "Your daughter was arrested with four other suspects including Jessica Hampton, Jane Kingston, Robert Benson and Josh Brown. Do you happen to recognize any of these names?"

Helen Goodall frowned. "Jane Kingston is our neighbors' daughter but Carrie has always told me she is a very down-to-earth and good girl. As for the others, I've never heard of them."

Good, my foot. Alison shot her sister another look and instead of responding with one of her signature glares, Carrie looked defeated and weary. She gave Alison an apologetic look before looking down at the table again.

"Alison?" Her mother turned to her. "Do you know the others from school?"

"Well, I.." Alison stammered.

She could feel Carrie's gaze creeping on her skin. When her brown eyes met Carrie blue ones, she suddenly felt this sense of regret. If only she had told her parents about Carrie's issues, her sister wouldn't have wound up being arrested and running a possibility of being persecuted. She was responsible for Carrie's predicament. She hadn't been a good sister. Alison was afraid to tell on Carrie in the initial stages because Carrie might spill the beans on Edward and towards the end, she feared that the revelation will make Carrie angry so she didn't do anything.

I'm such a fool.

"Alison, don't blame yourself," Carrie whispered. She looked like a fourteen-year-old again, vulnerable and in need of protection and Alison, being the big sister, was supposed to be the protector. She unwittingly ended up being the evil witch, the villain who spoilt everything for everyone. No wonder Edward didn't want her.

"No, it's my entire fault. You're here because of me," Alison sobbed.

"Don't say that. I was just too naïve. I shouldn't have trusted Jane. I should have believed you," Carrie muttered. "Jane betrayed me in the end. Alison, you must believe me-" she begged. "I didn't do drugs. Jess and Jane were the ones who went on high taking that stuff at Josh's party. They offered it to me but I refused. I really didn't know how the drugs eventually ended up in my pocket. I'm sure that Jane was the one who implicated me. She must have acted on Jess' orders. You're right, Ali, she's a bitch," she cried out.

"Language!" Her mother snapped immediately, as if preventing her daughter from swearing was an important priority right now.

Endless thoughts swirled within Alison's mind. "Jess and Jane set you up?" she asked disbelievingly.

"Yes, I swear. They did the urine test but it was positive. I didn't take drugs, I really didn't !" Carrie howled in a hysterical voice. Officer chick came over and pinned her down on the table and Helen Goodall finally snapped.

"You take your hands off my daughter," she demanded angrily.

"Stop it!" Alison moaned, putting a restraining arm on her mother.

"SIT DOWN!" Officer Dude commanded loudly and everyone quieted down. This cop really had a subduing effect to him.

"Miss Goodall, from your conversation just now, I'm assuming you know who the suspects are?" Officer dude turned to Alison now and he frowned. She could totally see his mind nitpicking and running through the details of what Carrie and she had said. She might as well give in.

"Yes, I do know all of them. Jessica is the head of the Mean Girls' Gang," Alison started.

"Ali! You can't tell them this stuff!" Carrie said, horrified.

Alison shook her head. "It's no use now. We've to tell the police everything."

Carrie slumped back in defeat. Even Alison could tell that Carrie couldn't come up with some clever plan to bail herself out. There was nothing left to do but reveal everything about the MGG and the BBG. There was a thing one must know. It was the unspoken rule in Cornwall Institution that no one spoke of the existence of the MGG and the BBG. Like the prime minister, they're invisible yet they wield a huge amount of authority and no one ever dared to cross their path by telling people about their illegal activities- well, at least, no one until now. Alison was sure that Carrie and she were one of those few people who were trapped in the most unusual circumstances and she had enough of the MGG's snobbish attitude and how they evoked fear in people. It was time to end it and it wasn't as if she had much of a choice.

"Well?" Officer Dude demanded impatiently.

"In our school, we have two gangs, the Mean Girls' Gang and the Bad Boys' Gang," Alison continued more confidently. "Jessica is the leader of the former while Robert is the leader of the latter."

"Are they street gangs?" Officer Dude wrote down something in his navy blue notebook.

"They aren't that simple. I think street gangs are usually formed for fun sometimes but as far as I know, Jessica's father is the famous Andrew Hampton and everyone knows he is a powerful man. It is a rumor," Alison stressed. "- and I don't know how true it is, that her father paid a lot of money or had some hold on the school's administrative committee such that the teachers included pay a blind eye to all their activities."

"Activities? Can you specify some of them?" Officer Dude looked really intrigued now.

Alison racked her head, trying to fish out some information which either Angela or Alex had said. But at this moment, Carrie's strangled voice rang out loud and clear.

"Drugs is one of their forte. Andrew Hampton smuggles drugs, both in and out of the country."

"You do realize that lying is a criminal offence in the eyes of the judge," Officer Dude warned with a piercing look.

"It's the truth," Carrie insisted adamantly, with more vigor then before. "I once overhead Mrs. Hampton told Jess during our monthly sleepover that her father was arranging a meeting the next morning with some of the drug syndicate dealers. Jess asked why was her dad engaging in these illegal activities and her mother replied, "How the hell are we supposed to afford all these luxuries then?". I was so scared that I just hid in my bedroom."

"Anything more?" Officer Dude was scribbling furiously now and there was a glint in his eyes. Alison had a feeling that he was the type of guy who sought after adventure.

"This might be hard to believe but..." Carrie winced. "Jess and Jane are streetwalkers."

Alison could hear her mother draw in a sharp rasp of breath. "Why would they do that?" Alison found herself asking, not exactly comprehending the situation.

"They do it for the "thrill". Every time we skipped class, they'll head over to one of the pubs and hook up with some guy. They even tried to convince me to do it."

"Did you do it?" Officer Chick asked. She was practically hanging on to Carrie's every word.

"Mabel," Officer Dude barked. "Sorry, sir." Embarrassment colored Officer Chick's cheeks.

"Did you do it?" Alison repeated the question.

"Yes," Carrie whispered with only a moment of hesitation. "But only once, I swear."

Hearing her answer, Helen Goodall stood up quickly and knocked over her chair but she didn't even notice. "Carrie Goodall, I'm utterly disappointed in you," she snarled and slapped Carrie twice- leaving a red palm mark on her daughter's face. Carrie was in mortified shock as she shook and fell onto the ground, her legs having turned into jell-o.

"No! Mother, don't!" Alison screamed. She rushed to help Carrie up but Officer Chick got there before she did. "Sit up," Officer Chick instructed sternly and shoved Carrie roughly back to her seat.

"Both your father and I trusted you so much but you created all these trouble for s," her mother uttered angrily. "How the hell did you become like this? You weren't like this in Japan!"

"I'm sorry, Mum, I'm so sorry…" Carrie wailed as her childlike face twisted into a picture of sorrow.

"Mrs. Goodall, would you PLEASE calm down?" This time, Officer Dude looked really pissed. "I'm sure you don't want to end up being put in handcuffs as well." He meant it. Alison saw that Officer Chick's hands were practically itching to the cuffs she had locked onto her belt. She frowned.

Her mother didn't sit down but instead, jabbed a finger in the direction of Carrie. "Will she be prosecuted?"

"Yes, madam," Officer Dude said regretfully. "I'm afraid, underage streetwalking is illegal and in spite of your daughters' claims, our lab tests have come back, proving that she did consume drugs and hence, she will be bearing two charges to her name. But if she is willing to testify in court, she might get a lighter sentence. For the time being, she'll be on probation."

Alison observed Carrie carefully. Her sister was in midst of digesting all these and she bowed her head down. Her impassive face showed no signs of sadness but only acceptance of her fate. Her mother seemed as if she was about to cry but couldn't. Only Officer Chick looked visibly unconcerned.

"Thank you for your cooperation. As for the involvement of Andrew Hampton, we'll conduct another investigation for this to verify the validity of your statements and we'll not contact you until further notice," Officer Dude said in a monotone voice but he sounded disappointed, as if he was putting down a book after reading pages after pages of a good story.

"Is my sister granted bail?" Alison asked hopefully and Carrie gave her a grateful glance.

"Yes, she is, but we'll need one of her parents to sign the form. I assume that Mrs. Goodall..?" he trailed off uncertainly.

"Mother? Let's post the bail and just bring Carrie home?" Alison tugged her mother's sleeve, feeling like a six-year-old kid making a request again. Her mother's body remained immobile and unmoving at her touch.

"Mrs. Goodall, the police's time is precious, would you like t-" Officer Dude repeated.

"No, I'll not be posting bail for my daughter," Helen Goodall interrupted coldly.

"But Moth-"

"Mu-".

"Speak no more, my decision is final. Carrie needs to learn how to pay for her mistakes." With that, Helen Goodall stormed out of the room in a flourish, ignoring the pleas and leaving both her daughters staring after her- one looking ashamed and the other looking stupefied.

***

"Mother, wait up!" Alison weaved through the streams of people just to catch up with her mother whose footsteps were quickening. At this rate, she wouldn't be able to make her stay and convince her to bail out Carrie. There was no way her mother would want to torture her own daughter by letting her rot in the cold prison cell for several nights when there was a much better alternative option.

Some people stared at her curiously. Normally, she would be disturbed by the fact that she was the focus of everyone's attention but for now, nothing was more important than saving Carrie.

Suddenly, her mother stopped. She was staring at someone straight ahead. Alison practically sped through the corridor and her heart almost stopped when she caught sight of someone.

No, a family, would be more specific. The entire Kingston family was in the waiting area. Edward was there too. Alison could feel her blood curdle with trepidation after registering this startling fact. All the Kingstons looked up when they spotted Alison and her mother. There was a mixture of emotions of their faces and none of them were pleasant.

Mr. Kingston gave them a courteous and rueful smile while Mrs. Kingston turned away as she dabbed at her cheeks with her flowered embroidered handkerchief. Alex waved at her cheerily. He was bending over the latest adventure flick book on Jackie Chan. Alison smiled back and her eyes inevitably shifted to the stone figure next to him. She sighed.

Edward was staring blatantly at her and a deep "V" frown creased over his forehead. There were shades of dark eye rings and he had his five-o-clock shadow, a sign that he hadn't shaved. He almost looked like a tramp, well, close enough if you count resembling a gutted homeless person who could be a model at the same time. Edward looked suspicious as his glance flickered between Alex and her simultaneously. She realized she hadn't told him about Alex but this was not the best time to talk as everyone would attest to.

Helen Goodall noticed Edward and she nodded to her daughter. "Aren't you going to go over to say hello to your boyfriend?"

"Maybe, next time," she murmured, inviting a disapproving glare from her mother.

Suddenly, a cop led a disheveled-looking girl out to the waiting area. "Jane Kingston," the cop announced. There were gasps of delight emanating from the matriarch and a sigh of disappointment from the patriarch. Alex and Edward merely shrugged indifferently. "Oh, Jane!" Mrs. Kingston's embraced her daughter, her bony figure crushing against Jane's soft body.

"Snuff it, Mum, this is sooo embarrassing," Jane winced, pulling away. Mrs. Kingston looked hurt but she added brightly, "Let's go back, now! I've an apple crumble in the oven, which I know it's your favorite dessert..."

"Hang on a moment," Mr. Kingston said sternly. "Jane, we're not going home until you explain everything fully to us."

"Gosh, Dad, can't you be a freaking less uptight." Jane rolled her eyes.

"Both your mother and I have given you too much leeway," he continued loudly. "How many times have you been arrested?"

"John!" Mrs. Kingston shook her husband urgently. "It's no use telling her that now. Let's go home." Her eyes flicked across the room. The raised voices had attracted the attention of several people, including the police officers who made no move to interfere. They were all clearly enjoying a good show.

"Paula, can't you see it? We've spoilt our daughter!" Mr. Kingston exploded. "It's all because of us she got into so much trouble even though she's only fourteen this year, fourteen!"

"You can't blame her. It's all because of the bad influence of her best friends." With this, Mrs. Kingston shot Alison and her mother an accusing look, as if blaming them for introducing Carrie to Jane.

"Don't accuse the Goodalls," Mr. Kingston hissed back. "You know very well that Jane was the one who brought Carrie astray. If anyone is in the wrong, it's us."

"Benjamin! How can you say that of our daughter?"

"Look at Jane, she's atrocious. She's a fine example of our bad parenting. What have you got to say for yourself?" Mr. Kingston retorted, his usually calm face rippled with anger.

Alison gaped openly at the sight. A lot of people were surrounding them now and everyone craned their necks to find out what was happening. At this moment, Officer Dude arrived and he broke into the circle and said, "Clear off now. Please do not make a scene here."

"Let's go," Mr. Kingston conceded and marched towards the door. As he passed by Alison, he murmured, "I'm sorry for your sister. It is Jane's fault and I'll make sure she would be taken into hand." Before Alison could reply, Mr. Kingston had moved on and he was gone. Mrs. Kingston put a hand around Jane who shook it off.

As Jane passed by Alison, she sneered under her breath, "Carrie Goodall got her just desserts. She didn't even realize I slipped something into her vodka last night. Such a dimwitt," Alison opened her mouth to retort but closed it again.

"You, young lady, you'd better steer clear from my daughter or else," her mother hissed to Jane as she walked past her despite the latter's nonchalant attitude.

And then there were two. The brothers walked next to each other, visibly uncomfortable with the close proximity to their sibling. Alex grinned and thumped her on the back.

"Yo, Ali."

"Hi, Alex," she breathed.

Only the elder brother stopped. He continued staring at her with no shame and Alison looked down. Alison's mother noticed the tension and she spoke, "Hello, Edward, such a pleasure to see you."

"Hello, Mrs. Goodall, " Edward answered coolly. "Nice to see you too."

"Things are alright between you and my daughter?" Her mother sounded mildly interested.

He hesitated after a tiny beat of silence. "Yes, we're both fine-" he turned to her. "I hope."

"Hmmm," Alison hummed in a low voice as she pretended to be interested in an ant on the floor.

"Meet me at the Lakeside Restaurant at 5pm tomorrow," he lowered his voice.

"Mmmm," she mumbled accommodatingly and Edward walked towards the door, but not before casting a brief longing backward glance at her.

"Alison," her mother started.

"I know. I know. I won't meet him tomorrow since I don't have your permission," Alison answered wearily.

A smile twitched on Helen Goodall's face. "On the contrary, I was hoping we could hit the malls."

"For what?" It seemed like a weird occasion to go shopping and Alison wasn't in the mood either. Although she had recently made up with her best friend, her relationship with her boyfriend was on the rocks and her sister was in custody.

"Come on, don't you youngsters always tell us adults to chill out?" Her mother grinned, looking ten years younger and showing Alison a glimpse of her youthful playful side. "We're going to select an outfit so that you can dazzle your boyfriend," she declared.

****

Parents

Next day.

Alison was having serious second thoughts about being a Barbie Boll guinea pig. Her mother had spent the entire day (8 hours straight, she had counted) trimming her hair, making adjustments to her outfit and playing with her age-old Chanel makeup. But she had a sinking feeling that she was about to look like a badly dressed geisha the moment she saw herself in the mirror.

It was probably worth it though. Although her mother's happiness came at the expense of her comfort, she was glad to see her mother's spirits lift especially after that terrible row last night. Alison had gotten up at around midnight to get a glass of milk but she heard loud voices coming from her parents' bedroom and there were loud thumping noises. If she were anyone else, she would probably have called the police, thinking that a murder had taken place and her father had dragged her mother's dead body to be buried in the woods. However, she was someone who understood her parents so she merely went back to bed, fully well knowing that her mother would still rise up early the next day looking energetic and upbeat and her father would be in his usual I-can't-be-awake-without-my-Starbucks-coffee mood even if both of them were engaged in a cold war which was frankly, quite a relief. That particular morning, the seat next to her felt empty, because its occupant was miles away in a prison cell and probably watched over by that sadistic Officer Chick but Alison held on to the fierce hope that Carrie would be able to emerge victorious over these trials and tribulations. For now, she would concentrate on preparing for "The Talk" tonight with Edward.

"I think blue eye shadow would go nice with your dress," her mother said as she rushed off to rummage through her make-up kit.

"Sure," Alison said accommodatingly.

Her mother came over and fingered the pearls. "This was my wedding present from your grandmother." Helen Goodall's eyes went misty as she tried to recall the past.

"Wow," Alison echoed. "Are these pearls real?"

"I think so." Her mother applied some red blusher to her cheeks. "I'm giving it to you now."

"Why are you giving me something so precious?" Alison asked doubtfully.

"You're my daughter. Who else would I give it to?" her mother answered. "Now, should we try the pink or red lipstick?"

"But Mu-Mother," Alison cut in. "Shouldn't you give this to Carrie?"

"Why?" Her mother was momentarily distracted as she tried to mix some of the lipsticks together to get a rouge brownish color.

"I mean...." She was forging into dangerous territory now but she just couldn't stop. "Isn't she your favorite daughter?" The unspoken assumption was now out and her mother lifted her head up in surprise at her words.

"What do you mean?" her mother repeated.

"Mother, you don't need me to tell me, but I'm well aware that Carrie has always been more favored," Alison answered exasperatedly. "It's hard for me to live with but I can accept it." She turned away almost immediately, knowing fully well that she might earn a hard-dealt slap in return.

"I think you're mistaken, Alison." Her mother frowned and put down all her makeup tools. "Is that what you have been thinking all these years? Tell me honestly."

"Yes," Alison whispered.

"Do you honestly believe that I'll be biased?"

"But Mu-Mother, it's the truth."

Her mother closed her eyes and spoke slowly, "I won't deny that we shower both love to Carrie but that is because she's a youngest child. After yesterday's incident-" With this, her lips pressed into a hard line. "-it has more than proved that you're much mature then your sister and we trust you, that's why we rely on you to take of yourself more."

"But, what about Father?" Alison whispered. "He hates me."

"Your father loves both of you a lot but he's a man who does not show his feelings directly," her mother continued. "You might not know it but we had a huge tiff because he was expecting a son and he was disappointed that we ended up with two daughters."

"He was?" Alison was stupefied.

"I don't think he has ever gotten over it but he has come to appreciate both Carrie and you. You should try and understand him. Your father is a good man, maybe he's not perfect, but he's definitely much better than some of the men I've seen," her mother laughed.

"Well…"

"You'll understand it one day when you establish a family with Edward," Helen Goodall said wistfully.

"Mother!" Alison yelped. What was all this talking about marrying Edward? Although it was a rather nice idea (she would love to see him in a tuxedo), she thought it was hardly appropriate to talk about marrying a guy when she was only sixteen.

"Oh, Alison," her mother's face wrinkled into a grin. "You might not have noticed it but Edward really has it for you."

"We've only dated for three months. For all you know, it's probably just a short-lived romance." Alison shrugged. It was a rather disturbing thought but from the limited experiences she had with boys, she knew that their attention span and liking for a girl was extremely short. Edward might not seem like such a guy but she wouldn't be honestly surprised if he ended up hooking with Jessica or someone like that.

"Please, I've been in so many relationships before I met your father," her mother argued as she tried fiddling with the lipgloss. "This Edward kid is really intense about you. You can tell it just by looking at his eyes when he looks at you," she paused dramatically. "-the most important question is, are you serious about him?"

"I am. I really do like him." Who wouldn't? After all, he had so many uncountable attributes: sweet, charming, delightful….

"Do you love him then?" Her mother had proceeded on to drawing her eyebrows.

That question caught Alison off-guard. "How am I supposed to know? I'm only sixteen. I've no idea what love is," she replied slowly, twirling the last word with her tongue. The word tasted so foreign. True, it was such a common word she often encountered in many romance stories but she had never ever applied this…word to herself.

"You can love someone when you're sixteen," her mother hesitated, her hand paused in midair. "I met my first love when I was eighteen and I wasn't any much older than you are right now."

"Father wasn't your first love?" Alison was astonished.

"That is reality. I remembered how fanatic I was about this guy and we almost talked about getting hitched out of high school," her mother muttered. "But it wasn't meant to be. He was whisked off to Alaska to attend university because his parents wanted to keep him away from me."

"That's sad," Alison winced.

It was funny how she kept discovering new stories and sides to her mother only after she had arrived in America. She remembered back in Japan, she didn't talk much to either of her parents and the only casual conversation they had was during dinnertime with simple questions like: "How's your day" or maybe "Have you made any new friends in school?". During those times, her parents worked a lot harder than they did now and the Japanese curriculum was more rigorous so she rarely got to see, not even to say speak properly to them.

"Maybe things will end up well for Edward and you or maybe not but I'm quite relieved to say that this guy you have chosen is a nice boy." Her mother arranged her hairstyle and placed a hairpin to keep a stray strand of hair in place.

"Who were you expecting me to date then?" Alison asked sarcastically as her mother made touchups to her hair. "Some guy with tattoos?" It was an entertaining thought but Alison was rather sure that if she had chosen Alex to be her boyfriend; her mother would be more averse to the idea.

"Hopefully you won't," she wriggled a finger at her. "As long as you're happy, both your father and I would be happy so long as you don't engage in intimacy before you're a legal adult..."

"Don't bother me with all that sex talk!" Alison groaned. This was so embarrassing to even think about doing it with Edward.....Still, she wouldn't mind kissing that soft lips of his or stroking his tanned skin.... Alison almost slapped herself. She was behaving like some typical hormonal teenage and she definitely wasn't one. But she still couldn't help thinking....

"I won't. There you're done," her mother stepped out of the way, leaving Alison to judge for herself and see her reflection in the mirror. Her outfit was the emerald green dress she had previously bought for the Cornwall Institution's annual school dance (she still shuddered every time she thought of that) and her mother's heirloom, the long pearl necklace, was clasped around her neck. She was wearing silver ballet flats and her hair was curled and let down like a brown blanket.

"Isn't this a bit over the top?" She wondered if it was appropriate to dress like that and meet Edward when they were supposed to be discussing some serious stuff.

"The Lakeside Restaurant isn't just any dinky restaurant. It's the most expensive one currently opened in Seattle," her mother retorted. "They wouldn't let you in even if you turn up in the best tailor-made kimono."

Alison was just about to laugh when all of a sudden, her mother clasped a hand over her mouth. "Oh no! I forget to hand a letter to you that came in the mail a week ago," she rambled.

She almost chuckled. It was just typical of her mother to forget things like that. What letter could it possibly be? Her curiosity was aroused.

No one had ever sent her a snail mail in America before except for official mailings from Cornwall or the occasional advertisements and surveys.

"There's no time!" Her mother cried out as she looked at the owl clock in her bedroom. "It's 4.30 already."

"The date's only at 5pm...." She wanted to delay the thing as far as possibly.

"I'll give you the letter some other time." She hurriedly pushed Alison out of the door.

"How am I supposed to get there anyway?" Alison asked as they emerged into the living room. It wasn't her mother's style to let her take the tube and get the dress messed up.

"Your father's taking you."

Alison's blood chilled. She found her rigid father standing by the door like a frozen block of ice. She gulped. No way, she didn't want to get into the car with him and despite her mother's constant reminders and her frequent reassurances to try and foster a close relationship with him, she just couldn't imagine herself being all chummy with....him. Okay, fine, her father.

"Since when do we have a car?" she squeaked.

"Your father rented it for the day." Her mother hurriedly gave her the onceover check and smiled satisfactorily.

"All ready to go?" her father asked gruffly, not even bothering to take a look at her as he clasped the car keys tightly in his big rough hands.

"Mother..." Alison hinted.

"You promised," her mother reminded again. "Now, just go. It's not good to leave Edward waiting there."

Oh no. She really was going to get slaughtered soon.

By her own father, no doubt.

****

Alison sat silently in the car and her hands had turned clammy by the time they turned out of the driveway. The silence was practically crushing her and she suddenly felt the overwhelming need to make some conversation but she couldn't come up with any topics. A scratch old record from the local radio station was flowing musically from the speakers.

"How's school for you now?" her father unexpectedly asked. Alison took a peek at him. His eyes were still on the road and he made no eye contact with her, for which she was thankful for.

"Great. I...er... made some new friends along the way." Alison didn't mention that she was already at Cornwall for three months but seeing as how this was the first actual conversation she was forced to engage in with her father, she figured she had better keep her father up to date starting from Day 1.

"The Alex lad?" Her father didn't sound too happy. Maybe he was still angry over Carrie's incident.

"Yes. I'm also friends with Angela Weber. Her parents open a grocery shop at 4th Street Avenue."

"The Webers," her father answered approvingly. "Respectable bunch."

"Uhuh," Alison said irritably. Who really cared whether your friend's family was "respectable" or not? The next thing she knew, her father might be telling her to start talking to people like Jessica because her family was rich.

"Are you coping well?" her father sniffed.

"Okay," she answered. "Edward helps me out sometimes."

"The Kingston boy," he said a little awkwardly.

"Yes, the Kingston boy," she answered. It was getting a little annoying. Her father was always just stating the obvious.

"Fine lad."

"Yes, he's a very decent boyfriend if that's what you mean."

"I trust you but don't mess around, or else," he cocked his head to the side to give his famous evil eye. Alison shuddered and nodded obediently.

"Edward's old-fashioned. He wouldn't do anything reckless," she defended.

"I can tell."

Alison couldn't discern whether that was a compliment as well. This time, she took a longer peek at her father. As a kid, she used to be so scared of him that she didn't dare to even speak to him in the face and that fear still lingered even when she reached teen hood. Even with that, she secretly respected her father. He commanded authority in a way like a dictator and his demeanor was really compelling at times though he inspired fear as well. It was unusual for her to witness how he had aged. Fifteen years ago, he was a dashing American man with floppy brown hair over his eyes who was ready to move out of his small town in Texas just to further his ambitions. When her mother first showed Alison her parents' wedding photo, she was so surprised to see her father smile in the picture. And quite surprisingly, her father's smile was heartwarming and genuine and even his eyes twinkled. That was when Alison could really sense his happiness and joy when he married her mother. After years of laboring, the hard times had hardened his character and he no longer smiled as much, perhaps even ceasing smiling at all. Still, Alison wished she could catch a glimpse of him smiling in real life- just once would suffice- but there wasn't a chance to begin with.

"What're you looking at?" Shit, her father was looking at her and he seemed terribly uncomfortable She hurriedly shifted her gaze to the windscreen.

"Nothing si-I mean, Father." When she was young, she remembered her father teaching Carrie and her to address him as "sir" until her mother put her foot down and demanded him follow everyone else on this planet and allow his own daughters to call him the normal way which was just plain old Dad. It had become a practice for her up until the age of nine so she slipped sometimes even now.

"Your mother has told you that I've given approval for you to date this Edward boy so you need not worry," he continued as stiffly as ever.

"Yes, and I truly appreciate that." Alison didn't like speaking in such an Old English way but her father always insisted for her to be polite. It wasn't too difficult back in Japan because everyone behaved in a similar fashion but America was a different thing. She really had to adjust her language pattern because she caught people giving her strange looks in school.

"How're you going to manage when this Edward person goes to California in weeks' to come?"

"I honestly don't know," Alison said truthfully. This was something they didn't discuss and Alison certainly wasn't going to tell Edward that she wasn't confident in continuing a long distance relationship and she was truly hoping to work out a solution.

"Settle this soon. You don't want to wait for him for so many years until he graduates." Her father ignored a driver who was swearing some colorful language at him because he had cut his way.

"Yes, I'll get onto it," she replied brusquely, sounding more like his receptionist than his daughter.

For a moment, each one of them stared away uncomfortable. Suddenly, her father asked, "Has your mother told you about the scholarship?"

"What scholarship?" Alison asked carefully.

"You'll know sooner or later." There was an ominous tone to his voice.

"If it concerns me, I would like to know," she answered. "Now."

Shooting her a vicious look, her father frowned before swerving efficient past a black SUV. She swore the driver inside made a "L" sign at her father but as usual, he was unperturbed. "Your mother said that it would be more appropriate if she speaks to you herself."

"Just tell me, I've the right to know," she asserted, surprised that she hadn't backed down or cowered in fear but then again, being in

America somewhat changed her and she didn't feel the need to listen to everything her parents' said. She learnt to question a lot of things and her mother would say it was bad attitude but she appreciated the change. It allowed her to be more confident.

"Your Japanese school sent us a letter to tell us that you won one of their scholarships to go to auniversity."

"But I left the school already…"

"The headmistress mentioned that yours would be a case of exception and that you would be eligible for it as long as you choose to attend a Japanese university the moment you leave high school at the age of eighteen.

"You mean… I've to return to Japan again if I accept it?" she questioned, sounding unusually baffled.

"Weren't you very enthused about going back to Japan some day?" her father asked suspiciously. "You gave us the impression that you didn't like America."

Alison shook her head slowly. She didn't know why but now, the option of going back to Japan didn't seem so appealing to her. It was true that integrating herself into the American community was hard and it took some getting used to but she felt that she belonged here now. Even if she only needed to leave at eighteen, she would feel horrible for leaving behind her friends, Angela and Alex, and most of all....Edward. It was funny, but the three-month-old relationships she had fostered with her American friends were nowhere as strong as the ones she had in Japan, even with her best friend, Etsuko. And the thought of returning to the other side of the globe and being so different from the others there really put her off.

"I...don't know, I'm really confused," she admitted.

"The scholarship is really prestigious. You might want to consider it," her father said neutrally. "Does Mother want me to go?"

"Helen is fine with it. She's really thrilled." His voice only hid a slight injection of disapproval. "Of course, she would prefer if you could attend an American college but given our finances, perhaps, going to Japan might be a better option."

"And you?" Alison blurted. She didn't know what made her ask for his opinion. After all, if given her way, she would prefer to not consult him but she needed to know his opinion. It was as if without his input, she would not feel comfortable of going ahead with any decision she made.

"Me?" He sounded genuinely astonished. "Since when do you care what I think?"

Hello, he's not as clueless as I think. Alison thought before coughing inconspicuously and recited theatrically, "It is only the duty of the daughter to seek permission from her parents before making a decision." She almost grinned when she saw the squeamish look on her father's face.

"Hm," he continued staring ahead and without any much effort, he cruised past the red light. "It is a great opportunity for you but I would prefer it if you could grow up and live in America," he answered.

"Why?" Alison was morbidly curious.

Her father paused. "I know how it feels like to start all over again in a new country and I do know it has been hard on both of you sisters. I was a youth in Texas who was in a hurry to get out of the stuffy climate and to shake off the annoying Texan slang but when I arrived in Turkey, I lost myself. I started to miss home a lot even if there was no one waiting for me back in America," he cackled and Alison almost jumped at the sound of his voice.

"So you think I shouldn't go?" she asked cautiously.

"You can but you need to ask if you're willing to give up everything here. I will tell you that the reason why we returned back to the States was because your mother and I got so sick of living abroad that we still ended up back here even when both Helen and I originally resented living in America," her father muttered.

"I see." Alison couldn't believe she had one entire conversation which lasted 17 minutes exactly (she counted) but her father's words actually made real sense.

"Remember, you can go back to Japan or some other place to travel or work but your heart will always be back in your homeland, here, even if you don't know it. Japan is a fine country, advanced technology and all of sorts, but do you really want to spend the best of your years in college in a country where you'll always be treated as a foreigner?" her father frowned. "Circumstances are the ones which push us to make certain decisions but family is the most important factor. We're here by the way."

The car jerked to a stop and her father turned to look at her, expecting her to get out.

"Thanks....Dad," she mumbled.

"No problem, my duty," he answered grumpily.

"Dad, let me give you a hug, will you?" Alison asked timidly.

If her father was surprised by her request, he didn't show it. "Whatever, I don't care."

Stretching out her arms, Alison wrapped them around his father in an awkward and somewhat reluctant embrace. Barely two seconds passed before her father pulled abruptly away looking all red-faced before mumbling, "You'd better get out of there."

"Bye Dad." Alison smiled and hopped out of the door and headed towards the restaurant. She didn't manage to witness it but she would have been proud had she seen a single drop of tear roll down her father's cheeks as he watched her leave.

***

Happily Ever After

Hang on, this is NOT the end. There's still one more chapter (Epilogue) and a sequel, YES, a sequel coming right up. Stay tune for more details on it!

The Lakeside Restaurant was an exclusive and luxurious restaurant which demanded all its customers to make reservations beforehand. It was situated beside a man-made lake whereby water activities like fishing and ski-ridding often took place. The restaurant's exterior was furnished in distinct colors with a combination of blue and silver.

Alison gulped as her turn came at the front of the queue. At the check-in point, she said nervously, "I need a seat, please." She was really nervous because the people behind and her were all decked in jewels and expensive night dresses. She heard one girl mutter, "I was expecting a 10 carat Tiffany ring but he gave me only a 5 carat one so I broke up with him!" It was terrifying to hobnob with the rich and the famous.

The Manager, who was busily checking people in, was impeccably dressed and his gold nametag read, "John Hopkins". He eyed her doubtfully and asked, "Have you made a reservation?"

"Ah, I haven't, but my boyfr-"

"No reservations, no entering," he answered bossily. "Next!" Alison was pushed out of the way but a bunch of giggling girls all wearing matching Christian Dior dresses.

"Please! I've a friend who is waiting for me," she whispered frantically.

"Ask your friend to come here then," the Manager sneered.

"But I don't have a mobile, I'm really meeting a friend here!" Alison wailed. A lot of people were staring her now. The group of look-alike girls were snickering and pointing at her. She could hear "Freak", "Weirdo" and some other less than flattering phrases hurled at her. She wanted to cry, sink down onto her feet or just bury herself in the bushes. She felt insulted, no, pissed, was the correct word. If only someone could save her from this socially embarrassing situation....

"Is there a problem?" A low, husky voice sounded out. A man stepped from inside the restaurant and he was staring at the commotion.

"Mr Kingston!" The Manager cried out. "Don't worry, it's just a frisky little girl trying to barge her way in. Rest assure, the moment your date, Miss Goodall comes, we'll notify you."

Edward was staring at her now and squinted his eyes. Alison got up to her feet. She should just run back home now. She didn't fit in with anyone. She didn't even deserve to be his boyfriend. As Jessica would say, she would never match up to him.

"Alison?" he murmured.

"No, I'm not, I..er...will just go." She should just run back home, call Edward and tell him that she was cancelling the date and that they had better not meet up because they were a mismatched couple. She was never in this league to begin with. Even those girls watching matching Gucci boots would be better suited for Edward than her.

But before she could scurry away inconspicuously, a strong arm grabbed her. "What the fuck are you doing?" he muttered.

"I...er..." There was a lump in her throat. The moment she saw him, she just couldn't be coherent anymore. No, not those hypnotizing blue eyes....

"Mr Hopkins, this," Edward pulled her closer to him. "-is my date. Now, will you please excuse her and let both of us enter?" he snapped unhappily.

"This is Miss Goodall?" The Manager's eyes bulged outwards, looking like a goldfish. All the other patrons were also tittering as they watched the scene goggle-eyed.

"Yes," Edward hissed and shoved the man out of the way, half-dragging Alison into the restaurant. Alison could barely believe her eyes. Inside the restaurant, its brightly-lit rooms with chandeliers stood out as uniformly-dressed waiters scurry past the tables whilst balancing dangerously stacked plates and cups with their hands (and sometimes on their heads). She tried to avoid knocking into a waiter.

"Sit here," Edward pushed her gently into a seat and she blinked. They were in one of those private rooms and the noise slowly faded out until the quietness took over.

"Now." Edward turned easily to her. "What on earth happened out there?" He sat down comfortably on one the plump chairs and folded his arms.

"That pompous manager almost threw me out because I was too shabbily dressed."

Something clicked in Edward's brain, she could sense it. An angry look passed over his face and he growled, snapping into his bad-ass mode, "I'll get a complaint letter in by tomorrow morning."

Alison didn't reply. She just stared at him. It felt strange to be so physically close to be after so long. They were sitting opposite each other at a ridiculously long table. He looked so dark and handsome and he was wearing a white polo shirt and black trousers and he smelt so good (his scent was always strawberry shampoo), as if he had just stepped out of the shower after bathing.

"Why the hell did you choose such an expensive diner to meet?" she demanded.

"You don't like it?" Edward gestured to the sparkling candle lights on the table. "I thought all girls love these things. A fancy restaurant, a candlelight dinner and sorts."

"Perhaps you don't understand me, after all," Alison said sullenly. This accentuated another one of their key differences. "What is it you want to talk about?"

Before Edward could answer, a waiter came in. "Mr Kingston, can I have your order now?" he asked professionally and his glance flickered to Alison only for a second but not before giving her a critical glance. Alison suddenly felt self-conscious and turned away, her face reddening.

"A bottle of red and two wine glasses please," he answered lightly and the waiter breezed out briskly again.

"The other day when you went all emotional on me," Edward began uncertainly. "You mentioned that you knew about Amber's... pregnancy. Are you pissed with me because of that?"

"Not really," Alison admitted. "I was just unhappy because you weren't honest with me."

"Believe me, I really wanted to tell you the truth but it's hard. How am I supposed to phrase those words anyway?" Edward mocked sarcastically. "Oh, hi, Alison, by the way, I got my ex-girlfriend pregnant and told her to abort it?"

"I didn't mean it like that." She frowned and crossed her legs nervously. "I...I just wanted to know why Amber aborted the baby and why you didn't end up with her as you should. Weren't you a happy couple?"

"You're mistaken, just like everyone else," Edward suppressed a grimace. "The "happy couple" thing was just a show we put on to give the impression. It was necessary for both of us. For me, I needed someone more...influential to depend on during high school. As for Amber-" his face hardened. "-she just made use of me to get attention and authority."

"But..." Alison looked confused and she stopped.

"Yes?" Edward stared at her. "What do you want to say?" he asked gently, careful not to startle her.

"Sorry, but I thought you were a nobody back in high school," she whispered. "Amber didn't need you."

Surprisingly, Edward didn't look the least offended. "She wanted me because of my looks and money. I was originally a nobody because of choice. I was careful to the point of being extreme such that I was suspicious of everyone wanting to be my friend. Until finally one day, I just got so angry about having no friends I ended up hooking up with her."

"Why didn't you keep the...the baby then?" Alison bit her soft lips. Edward wasn't any much older than her but to think of him as a father, it was quite hard to imagine. Mentally wise, he would make a great dad because he was so caring and responsible. But....physically wise, it was hard to imagine herself as a mother, let alone him as a parent.

"It's complicated." His face darkened as he furrowed his eyebrows in concentration. Edward kept tapping his fingers on the table, a move which Alison recognized as a sign of anxiety.

"It's okay, you don't have to push it and tell me, I understand," she said.

Edward replied wryly. "No, I want you to know. Ever since I declared my ardent love for you, I've been trying to seek an opportune time in order for me to tell you all my past and secrets except that it was hard for such topics to come up during a casual conversation."

"Hmm," Alison tried to disguise her astonishment at his proclamation with a cough.

Ignoring her, Edward continued, "When I first heard that she was pregnant, I didn't really feel that sense of happiness I was supposed to get when one knows that he is going to be a father."

"Maybe it was because you were too young so you were scared?" Alison offered.

"No," he shook his head. "It wasn't like that. She came to me and asked if we wanted to keep the baby but the sudden thought of spending the rest of my life with her put me off. The idea was downright terrifying. That made me realizes that I wasn't suited for her in the first place. I had never really treated her as my girlfriend."

At this moment, a knock came on the door. Both of them stiffened and waited as the waiter came in, put down the wine bottle and poured the red liquid into the fragile wine goblets before sailing out again.

"Have a drink," he gestured, picking up the glass itself.

"Minors can't drink," she retorted.

Edward grinned. "This is America, my dear. Don't tell me you haven't drunk alcohol in your life?"

"Only sake and that was only rice wine in Japan," she said defensively. When Edward shot her a look (which somehow, really resembled her father), she mutely took up the glass and swirled the red wine just like how people usually did in those old 80s movies.

He watched her action with great amusement and cleared his throat. "Her parents were terrified of course. They kept urging her to abort it but she didn't want to. My parents were shocked and they were utterly disappointed with me. I don't know how Dad and Mum managed to completely trust me again."

For a moment there, Alison got a flash of his real parents but the image soon changed to one of John and Paula Kingston. Of course he wasn't talking about his birth parents but his guardians, the same ones who loved and raised him. Alison finally understood the pain they must have felt when Edward committed this almost irreversible mistake.

"Both my parents respected my decision and I held the final decision. I don't know why Amber wanted the baby at first and I badgered her into telling me. It turned out that she thought that with the baby, she would be able to bind me to her forever," he said, his face became a picture of disgust. "After I confronted her, she agreed to do it."

Catching sight of Alison's discomfited face, he said, "This incident would always be a shadow. I wouldn't deny that I feel really guilty about destroying a life which I created myself. Sometimes, I just wished that I can turn back the time again." He released a melancholic sigh.

"And what? Have a baby with Amber again?"

"Obviously not." His face turned serious and intent. "I wished that I hadn't messed with Amber and maybe…my past wouldn't be tainted forever like that. That was before I met you. After falling in love with you, I kept wondering if I had met you earlier, maybe things would have turned out different."

"This is fate. We can't control things like that," Alison added softly. It strangely reminded her of what Etsuko once said, "It is no use to wish for something one can't have. Always remember that, Alison-san."

Funny how the same saying could be applied to two vastly different contexts.

"Will you forgive me Alison?" Edward's face was pained. "I knew that you were hung up about the virtue thing but I'm so sorry I did so many idiotic things in the past. You…you don't know how much I want the clock to turn back," he choked out and a single drop of tear streamed down his tanned perfect face.

Alison's eyes widened. He had never seen Edward cry and the remorseful and agonizing look he had made her want to sob too.

She reached across the table voluntarily and clutched his hand, "Edward, I forgive you. I was too childish and kept harping on stupid stuff like preserving your virtue and I'm going to correct that now. I wasn't here to share your pain three years ago but I'm here today just for that."

As if he couldn't help it, Edward managed a weak smile. "Alison, sometimes, I wonder how you can be so mature at the age of sixteen. At your age, I was still a fool who didn't know what to do with my life."

"Everyone's different. You can right this wrong as long as you try," she whispered.

"Miss Weber…Angela called me, you know." Edward stroked her skin with his long fingers.

"She did?" Alison looked up in amazement. "What did she say?"

"She told me a lot of stuff. It seems like she gave you a lot to think about," he mused. "She also explained some of the difficulties you faced. I never knew that living here in America could be so difficult for you at first."

"It's really all my fault," Alison said tactfully and took a little sip of wine. It tasted disgustingly bitter. " I needed time to readjust my values and thinking and I just had to learnt to be an American and not a Japanese."

"And were you successful in the end?"

Alison smiled. "I figured it didn't matter whether I was truly American or Japanese as long as I remain as myself and don't lose my own individual identity."

"So right," he murmured. "But I honestly promise that I'll try and consider your viewpoint as well. What Angela said was true, I've been an insensitive bastard. I didn't consider our differences at all."

"I believe you," she murmured and added, "So you're not mad at Angela for saying those secrets of yours? You aren't going to give her detention or anything, good o'Terror?"

"I am," he laughed. "But I'm also glad that she got the awkward part out for me. Girls are really better at approaching sensitive subjects. But you're seriously not at all bothered by the virtue"

"Did she tell you about your erratic tempers in class?" Alison couldn't resist asking.

"Well, I can't help if my mood swings happen to correspond to the ups and downs of our relationship," Edward said tenderly as he twirled his finger with her curly brown hair. "Nice hairstyle," he murmured appreciatively as he withdrew back to look at her more carefully. "Nice dress too."

"Thanks." Her face glowed. "Mother did all these for me. I think she went overboard."

"I don't think so." Edward smirked as his teeth grazed her skin. "By the way, how are your parents handling the issue with your sister?"

"Pretty well. They had a heated argument though."

"Understandably, I'm telling you, mine aren't that happy either."

"Are they okay then?"

"Mum kept blaming Carrie." He gave her an apologetic look. "But everyone else knows that we have put up with Jane for far too long already."

"Didn't they spot the signs of teenage rebellion much earlier on? Why didn't they stop it?" Alison asked, confused.

"Dad was all for getting a counselor," Edward looked bummed out. "But Mum insisted it was nothing and her darling angel daughter wouldn't do anything bad. Turns out she was wrong. Dad kept blaming himself that he should have took Jane in rein a long time ago. If not for my sister, your sister wouldn't have ended up in custody now."

"It isn't your fault. Carrie was in the wrong too."

"Just to tell you, Alex had a massive row with Mum. He almost threatened to move out if Mum kept shielding Jane and blaming both Carrie and you as a bad influence." Edward gazed at her curiously. "How come you never told me you guys made up again?"

Alison swelled up with pride. Good old Alex, sticking up for her as usual. He was indeed a worthy loyal friend. She replied, "We just reunited recently. I didn't get the chance to talk to you at all."

"And he isn't interested in you anymore?" Edward just looked a little jealous as he swigged another mouthful of wine.

"I think I made it pretty clear that if he dares to bring up his crush again, our friendship is off," she answered cheerily.

"That settles it then." Edward leant back and he looked positively relaxed as his fingers circled the ring of the wine glass. "All our problems are finally solved then."

"Edward..." Alison scrunched up her face. "I need to tell you something."

"What?" He suddenly turned alert again and narrowed his eyes.

"I...I receive a scholarship which I'm entitled to the moment I turn eighteen."

His anxious face dissolved into a genuine portrait of happiness. "That's great! Can you go to any university then? Why don't you go to Stanford? I would be able to meet you then by the time you graduated!" He said hurriedly as his mind flicked through numerous possibilities and plans.

"You got it wrong, Edward," she frowned. "I can only receive the scholarship if I go to a Japanese university and...it requires me to bond to a Japanese company and work there for a minimum of five years."

"What?" Edward looked staggered. "Doesn't that mean you'll be gone for an entire decade?"

"Give or take a year but yes." Alison's forehead creased with worry. "Do you think I should take it?"

"It's your decision of course," Edward tried to smile but couldn't. "I'm sure you'll get wonderful opportunities there and you'll have wonderful colleagues, friends, boyfriends..."

"Are you trying to ditch me?" Her voice rose by an octave.

"No," Edward said sadly. "I'm just saying, if that's what you want, I won't stop you. I'll still wait for you until you return back to America, no matter how it takes."

"Are you sure Edward? I'm after all, a rather insignificant high school girl. Surely some other future college girl would capture your interest," she said lightly but even she could detect the note of fear in her voice.

"There is no one else quite like you," Edward summoned his most mature voice. "I'm afraid that without you, I'll feel quite lost in my life," he said gravely. "I'm just trying to say that I won't be so selfish as to want you to sacrifice your dreams for me but just promise me, you won't go back to Japan and not return here again."

"I haven't decided yet. You don't have to get so uptight about it." Alison shrugged. "It still depends on… a lot of things actually."

"On what then?" His eyes flashed with interest.

"On certain circumstances," she echoed her father's words and raised her glass. "Let's just forget that for a while and enjoy this moment for ourselves."

"Now that's a thought." He raised his wine glass too.

"May we be together for as long as we're happy," she smiled.

"I'm all for it," Edward said enthusiastically.

They knocked the glasses together and Alison could practically feel the vibrations as the seconds passed. "I hope both of us honor that promise." She snuggled up against his chest, feeling warm and secure once more.

"Forever and ever," he agreed and kissed her.

THE END

***

Epilogue

"HAPPY BIRTHDAY ALISON!" Everyone screamed as they clapped and cheered.

"Thank-you," Alison whispered shyly.

She beamed at all the friends (and some strangers) who turned up for her birthday party which was jointly organized by Carrie and her. It was officially 18th December and her first birthday spent in America. Back in Japan, it was generally a quiet affair because their family didn't know a lot of people so the celebration was restricted to a small dinner with a few of her favorite dishes at a local restaurant. But this year, Angela came up with the idea to set up a birthday bash for her and everyone (including her parents) collaborated and chipped in. Many of the juniors and seniors were invited even if they didn't know her personally.

Speaking of Carrie, where was she? She casted a frantic glance around the room as a lot of people start to dissipate into little groups. Many people were hovering near the refreshments counter and a few came to give her well wishes but she felt vulnerable being alone.

"Hey, love." Edward strode up confidently and kissed her hair. "How are things?"

"Lovely," she smiled. "Any hot girls tried to pick you up?"

"One," he laughed. "I was too busy trying to fend off her amorous advances."

"Both Angela and Carrie went a little…extreme."

He gazed around the room disbelievingly. They had rented a big space (because Alison's apartment was too small) and had decorated it with many balloons, hand-made pompoms and countless sparkly fairy lights. In the middle of the room was the half-finished birthday cake which was designed in the shape of an American flag.

"Alison!" Carrie exclaimed excitedly as she came up behind her at this point. "Hey, I didn't see you there, Mr. Kingston, enjoying yourself?"

"It's Edward," Alison pouted. Her sister still hadn't kicked the habit of addressing his boyfriend as "Mr Kingston". It made her feel as if she was dating a much older guy.

"Sorry," Carrie apologized before asking cheerily, "Will I be addressing him as brother-in-law next then?"

"Maybe," Alison answered lightly, ignoring the surreptitious glances Edward was throwing her way.

"How's the first term at Stanford anyway?" Carrie turned to Edward.

"Brilliant. I love the courses there," he answered conversationally with his arms still wrapped around Alison. "Of course, I stole back to attend my girlfriend's birthday party. That can't be counted as illegal." He exchanged a knowing glance with Alison who giggled at his facial expression.

"Where's Alex anyway?" Alison asked as she twisted her head to look around.

"He's stuffing his mouth full of chocolate cake." Carrie put on a face. "Sometimes, I wonder how Angela can stand him."

"She's his girlfriend after all so she has to bear with him." Alison poked her in the arms and Carrie snorted.

It took a little getting used to after Alex announced he was going out with Angela. Alison wasn't surprised of course. She had long suspected Angela harbored more than just platonic feelings for her other best friend but she hadn't expected Alex to take the first step to court her. Angela was delighted of course but it was a little awkward at the start. All three of them initially had difficulty arranging time for their friends and romantic interests with a few tiffs along the way but they ended up making a pact to spend at least four hours each week with their buddies only.

Sometimes, Alison would have to admit that being with two friends who dated each other had its cons. She would stumble upon them kissing and undergoing some under-the-clothes action but thankfully, nothing more than that. As for Carrie, she declared that she had gotten over the short-lived crush on Alex and there were no more hard feelings between them even if...they had did it before.

"By the way, did you hear about the good news?"

"What?"

"I topped the entire junior cohort!"

"No way," Alison gapsed. "Really?"

"Yes! Principal Audrey was really pleased about it. She says that it's a fine turning around-" Carrie lowered her voice. "-especially after the incident.

"What's her problem?" Alison frowned. "Why does she keep reminding everyone of that? All of us just want to move on with our lives."

"Totally," Edward echoed dutifully, squeezing her arms. She wondered if he was even paying attention to the conversation.

As Carrie bounced off to chat with some of her mates, Alison couldn't help but feel relieved that the ordeal was finally over. Thankfully, Carrie wasn't charged for both offences (street walking and drug possession) although she was forced to go for counseling because the judge deemed her as a minor and worthy of a second chance. After a few regular sessions with a professional counselor, she managed to change her mindset and become more positive in her thinking and attitude before throwing herself feverishly back into school.

Under Principal Audrey's encouragement, Carrie also signed up for a few co-curricular activities. She swore off smoking, drugs, dyeing of hair, ditching of classes and tattoos (although the one of her forearm still remained). Both her parents were extremely happy after Carrie reverted back to her original self.

On the other hand, the rest of the Mean Girls' Gang's cronies ended up in a worse state. Jessica's parents were both charged for smuggling of drugs and her father was put behind the jail bars for seven years while her mother was let off for a lighter sentence of three years.

As for Jessica, she checked into a girls' rehab and she was currently still residing there. Jessica's entire family's vast assets were liquidated and sold off, leaving her with only a meager amount of inheritance. Alison almost pitied Jessica for coming to such a sad end. Both Robert Benson and Josh Brown (Angela's on and off ex-boyfriend) went to a boys' home but rumor has it that Robert's dad bribed someone to let his son go off on probation.

As for Jane Kingston, Alison had only seen her once ever since that incident and that was when she came back to collect her belongings. She didn't end up being sentenced to a girls' home because she had spun some elaborate tale to the judge about her being cheated and duped by Jessica.

Instead, after being let off, she chose to move out of her parents' home and accepted an offer to be an intern at some fancy office in New York after dropping out of Cornwall Institution. Edward once mentioned that her parents' hadn't received a single letter or e-mail from her and her father had almost given up hope of ever seeing his daughter again while his mother was adamant about Jane being "too busy to communicate".

The single biggest thing which happened in Cornwall Institution's history thus far was the dissolving of the Mean Girls' Gang and the Bad Boys' Gang. After the police interrogated the school committee and found out that Jessica's father had been donating a lot of money (or by saying it in a uglier fashion, bribing) the executive committee to pay a blind eye to everything and there was a big hoo-ha about it, many of the students wrote a petition and Principal Audrey finally outlawed them, destroying the so-called "special" cult status. It was sheer victory for many people, geeks especially, and a huge shock for many of the cheerleaders and jocks.

"By the way, where are your parents?" Edward murmured by her ear, tucking her brown hair behind her ear with one swift movement as Angela disappeared to talk to an old friend.

"They're out spending some quality time together," Alison chuckled. It was her idea that her parents start "re-dating" and get to appreciate each other more so that they can enjoy being alone with each other without any disturbances. Initially, they started out their dates simply by going to restaurants or bars.

Only recently did they proceed to doing more intense activities together like figure-skating. Alison almost laughed out loud as she imagined her father, a rather proud man, wobbling around the skating rink and hanging on to his dear life with her exasperated mother watching her husband, wondering why on earth she married him. Her parents were much happier now and she caught her father smiling twice so far. Alison decided to work harder to chalk up a higher record.

"I'm totally getting jealous now," Edward mumbled, leading her to a private corner.

"Why?" Alison asked quizzically.

"I want to us to be like your parents when we're forty," he grinned.

"Sure, we'll wait for our kids to plan all these activities for us then," she smirked.

"Make sure you don't become some wrinkled old lady by then."

"Well, you'd better not turn into some foul-smelling old man," Alison retorted.

"Hmm, I just realized I never got to asking you about whether you accepted the scholarship." He deftly wrapped his strong arms around her.

"I'm sure you know the answer," she teased, trying to ignore the fact that he had slipped his hand under her shirt. She had rejected the offer even after strenuous letters sent to her by her Japanese ex-principal.

She decided to remain in America and maybe continue on to an American college in the future (her father was exceptionally delighted) so that she could be near her friends, family and boyfriend. There was nothing left in Japan for her except for memories and it was simply pointless to return back there. Maybe someday, she would make a trip and tour around Japan but she knew that in the eyes of the Japanese, she would be the foreigner or the tourist. It used to bother her but it didn't matter now because she knew she had found her place in America, her homeland.

"By the way, I haven't given you a present here." Edward flashed a smile at her.

"I pretended not to notice."

"Here," Edward gingerly took out a silver locket from his pockets. The words "E & A" were carved on it in neat cursive handwriting. It was really stunning.

"Where did you get that?" Alison gawked at the pretty trinket.

"It belonged to my birth mother," he replied quietly. "This is the only memory I've of her."

"And you're giving it to me?" she asked disbelievingly. "Shouldn't you keep it for yourself?"

"No, I want you to have it." Edward carefully clasped the locket around Alison's neck and he sighed. "I love how it looks on you."

"Thank-you," she whispered. This was one of their special moments whereby nobody could disturb them unlike the other time when Alex accidentally-on-purpose stumbled into their room during an intense make-out session.

"I love you, Alison, I really do." He kissed her full on the lips, silencing her words and clasped his hands over hers. They were tangled together into one and Alison enjoyed the feeling of being touched by him immensely because his skin had a smooth, satin-like texture.

"I love you too, Edward." Alison smiled.

THE END

www.ingramcontent.com/pod-product-compliance
Ingram Content Group UK Ltd.
Pitfield, Milton Keynes, MK11 3LW, UK
UKHW020845120225
455007UK00010B/357